# THE GOOD OLD DAYS OF SHIPPING • WILLIA

CW01626901

**Publisher's Note**

The book descriptions we ask booksellers to display prominently warn that this is an historic book with numerous typos or missing text; it is not indexed or illustrated.

The book was created using optical character recognition software. The software is 99 percent accurate if the book is in good condition. However, we do understand that even one percent can be an annoying number of typos! And sometimes all or part of a page may be missing from the book. Or the paper may be so discolored from age that it is difficult to read. We apologize and gratefully acknowledge Google's assistance.

After we re-typeset and design a book, the page numbers change so the old index and table of contents no longer work. Therefore, we usually remove them.

Our books sell so few copies that you would have to pay hundreds of dollars to cover the cost of proof reading and fixing the typos, missing text and index. Therefore, whenever possible, we let our customers download a free copy of the original typo-free scanned book. Simply enter the barcode number from the back cover of the paperback in the Free Book form at www.general-books.net. You may also qualify for a free trial membership in our book club to download up to four books for free. Simply enter the barcode number from the back cover onto the membership form on the same page. The book club entitles you to select from more than a million books at no additional charge. Simply enter the title or subject onto the search form to find the books.

If you have any questions, could you please be so kind as to consult our Frequently Asked Questions page at www.general-books.net/faqs.cfm? You are also welcome to contact us there.

General Books LLC™, Memphis, USA, 2012. ISBN: 9781151464620.

PREFACE. IF a taste for antiquities was universal, how many interesting old vessels would have been saved to us. As a correspondent to *Fair Play,* June 27th, 1890, deplores—we take no care of our old ships, and excepting one or two historic men-ofwar, now well cared for, nor do we. Not only so, but were it not for that magnificent institution—the Library of the British Museum, even of the few records that remain of old time shipping, many would soon be lost.

It behoves us to do so, as each succeeding decade relegates the older existing type of vessel to the shipbreaker, while it brings us some new development in ship construction, her remunerative qualities being usually in inverse ratio to her graceful appearance. What possible resemblance can the "whale-back" monstrosity, or the "turret-decker," a hideous mass of iron, or rather steel, as absolutely devoid of grace and symmetry as she is (I trust) remunerative to her owners, bear to the traditional appearance of a ship.

Yet the metamorphosis has been comparatively gradual. The old frigate-built ship, with her square stern and quarter galleries, gave way to the clipper ship with the now familiar elliptical stern, to be succeeded by the iron clipper, again to be displaced by the huge steel "four-poster" of the present day. The early auxiliary steamers of fine form with lofty masts and square yards, succumbed to the fullpowered steamer with auxiliary sail power and now these are giving way to the modern steamship pure and simple.

The recent production in steam-shipping is but an enormous "lighter," the "whale-back" and the "turret-decker " to wit.

Yet even so, in this hard age of steam navigation, Kipling and others have discovered sentiment and even poetic interest, equalling that in the stories of the fleet clippers which so delighted our boyhood.

This book, I may preface, is the out-

collected during the past sixteen or seventeen years; and it is now about seven years since I conceived the idea of classifying and arranging them into book form. Then it was that I realised how utterly wanting were a few hundred notes of a finished book. Six pleasant months, however, in the Library of the British Museum, among the old Parliamentary returns, Board of Trade Tracts and Journals, &c, and newspapers of early date, some months in the Guildhall Library, London, the Glasgow Libraries, the Metcalfe Library, Calcutta, &c, &c, not only supplied confirmatory evidence to the notes but also much additional information.

Let me trust, however, that the reader is so interested in the subject of old ships as to condone the literary demerits of a work devoted entirely to them. The subject appeals to most of us; there are few men in whom there does not existan innate love of the sea, and so a veneration for the "oldtimers."

To the average individual, when viewing an old hulk or an old wreck, I am sure something more is suggested than that of a mere collection of wood or iron, worn out and falling into further decay. How much more interest attaches to the old fabric when regarded as a history in itself. The interest Ill which impels us to pause and reflect on the times in which the old ship was built; to speculate on the bright hopes which had induced the order for her building,—hopes resting on the probable need for such a vessel;—the intense excitement at her launch; the pride of the builder in his hand-work; of the owner in possession; and the succession of thought carries us on to the loading berth, when we fancy we can see her quaint advertisements in the newspapers of her date; and how, during her palmy days, her arrivals and departures are matters of public and, under some circumstances, such as conveying troops to the seat of war, of national importanceTime runs on, however, and does not spare the ship, but she is overhauled, restored and continues in the foremost rank. But, bye and bye there comes a time when the ship needs more repair than the owner cares to afford, and the ship, now getting old is, and possibly with reluctance. sold, succeeded doubtless by a larger and finer vessel. Her new owners perhaps run her on less liberal lines; her up-keep is scantier and she falls into a yet lower class and presently carries only inferior cargoes. The end is not far off now: foreigners yet may buy her, or she must be broken up or turned into a coal hulk in some far-off corner of the world.

Referring to the book itself, the greatest difficulty I have experienced has been the preserving of the continuity of a vessel's history. Her building is noted, and then she duly appears on the list of her owner's fleet; contemporary papers supply much of her history, supplemented by notices in foreign or colonial journals. Freight reports of her date, Government returns of the monies paid for the transport of troops, emigrants, convicts, stores, &c, also passenger lists give us her employment and possibly a clue to her succesS or otherwise, as a money-making machine. Matter of interest may be supplied by her owners or their descendants, some traditionary "yarn" may add to the interest of the vessel, and so we pursue her history until one day we find her name erased from the "Register." Unless she is associated with some well-known shipwreck, her further career now is hard to trace; possibly after some heavy repair she reappears on the Register, often under another owner and another name. Following her career, under the new ownership and name, years after perhaps, we again lose sight of her, to reappear in like manner, or may be, we notice the old vessel unhappily overdue and eventually posted as "missing," or perchance she be sold to foreigners where, under another flag and another name, it is almost impossible to trace her.

Steamers converted into sailing ships, cut in two to be reconstructed, supply instances of this difficulty. Some years back, when iron ships, ton for ton, cost more than they do at the present, it was no uncommon thing to hear of a ship cut in two, a bow put into one part and a stern into the other and appearing again as two vessels. That interesting periodical, the *Nautical Magazine,* in its issue of 1873, page 617, describes such a procedure: "The ""Lark," a paddle steamer, 210 feet long, 23 feet "beam and 10 feet 4 inches deep, of very light "plates and scantling, built of steel, supposed for "blockade purposes and registered in Liverpool "as the "Lark;" sold to foreigners and registered "in Liverpool as the "Port Said," having been "lengthened 60 feet, 8th December 1869, registered "owner John Roue Bickford of Liverpool; again "sold to foreigners, 1870, and registered in Liverpool as the "Hankow," 14th March 1870; again "owned by J. R. Bickford and re-registered at "North Shields, 8th March 1872, by John Robert "Kelso of North Shields. Since then she has been

"cut in two in Sunderland by the late Mr. William "Pile and converted into two screw steamships by "putting a new bow on one and a new stern on the "other—one the "Lilian," registered in London, "26th April 1873, as a new iron screw steamship, "built by W. Pile & Co., of Sunderland 1873; the "other is, we believe, lying in the Dock and in the "market for sale, but we cannot yet find any record "of her being registered. Both vessels we found "classed 75A. After the vessel was bought by J. R. "Kelso of North Shields, she was, in accordance "with the custom in such cases, reported as having "been broken up in 1872, and her registry as the ""Hankow" closed in the official books on the "24th September 1872."

The semi-historical character of this book has, of course, necessitated reference to many current periodicals, as well as standard works, and especially I must express my indebtedness to the *Nautical Magazine, Fair Play,* and *Notes and Queries.*

In nearly every case where I have transcribed, verbatim or otherwise, I trust I have duly mentioned the source; where I have omitted to do so, I trust that this may be taken as sufficient apology. The magnificent work of the late William Shaw Lindsay, I did not chance upon, until I was nearly ready to go to press. I find I have trodden somewhat (though very humbly) in his footsteps, as he quotes from many Parliamentary reports and returns which I also have seen and transcribed. His work is not only invaluable for reference, but exceedingly interesting; his own experience was considerable. Many old firms are not here represented; the great firm of "Wigram," Shipbuilders and Shipowners for example. I have had to compile, however, from material accessible to me. Steel's early lists mention the fine armed ships of Sir Robert Wigram—the "Glatton" of1,200tons and 38 guns; the " Nepturte" of 1,20a tons and 38 guns; the" Marquis of Ely " 1,200 tons and 36 guns, &c, &c, very far back in the century.

This book must not be judged from any literary standpoint. View it, courteous reader, as a "collector's" notebook, and the author as a" collector," continually endeavouring to unearth *antiente* records, and ever on the *qui vive* to bring to public notice, some interesting and rare specimen, yet afloat, (and there are yet a few) of early and mid-century shipping, and should it awaken in the elder reader any pleasant recollections, or present to the younger some few progressive phases of shipping in a more interesting light, the " collector " will not have deemed his note-book a labour in vain.

THE GOOD OLD DAYS OF SHIPPING. CHAPTER I. TN the year 1591, before the days of even quadrant J-or backstaff, a private venture was fitted out by an association of merchants, with a view to share in the much coveted wealth of the East Indies. Under one Lankester, there left England, three ships, of which but one ever accomplished the voyage, and that, after many vicissitudes. Commercially the enterprise was not a success, but the accounts of Captain Lankester were so hopeful that another expedition was ventured. A capital of £ 72,000 was speedily subscribed with which five ships were fitted out. The fleet comprised the "Dragon" the admiral's ship of the burthen of 600 tons, the "Hector" of 300, the "Susannah" and "Ascension" of 200 each, and the "Guest" storeship of 120 tons.,£45,000 was spent on their equipment, the remaining,£27,000 in purchasing such articles as were deemed the most advantageous for barter.

In the year 1600 the first charter was granted and more factories being established, the trade steadily increased until by 1679 eleven ships of 400 to 600 tons were employed, and four years later East India stock sold at,£500.

Old prints of these "waggons" shew them to have been fearful and wonderful crafts; castles were raised at both bow and stern for battle purposes and their sides simply bristled with guns, while the marvel is, considering their towering sides, their enormous castellated projections and their ill-cut bellying sails, not that they took so long to get to their destinations, but that they ever arrived at all.

As the account of this company pertains more to a History than to these pages, but a brief allusion shall suffice.

Pepys, in his quaint and interesting diary, describes how in 1665 he visited the India "shipp" "Sol on board my Lord Bruncker and there he "and Sir Edward Pooley carried me down into the "hold of the India shipp and there did shew me "the greatest wealth lie in confusion that a man "can see in the world. Pepper scattered thro' "every chink, you trod upon it and in cloves and "nutmegs you walked above the knees, whole "rooms full and silk in bales and boxes of copper "plate, one of which I saw opened. Having seen "this which was as noble a sight as I ever saw in "my life, I away on board the other shipp."

Such enormous profits reaped by a monopoly could not long continue without opposition, but the competing companies, which from time to time arose, generally amalgamated with the old company after a few years of fruitless competition.

In some of the earlier charters, the East India company was empowered to treat as pirates any unauthorised strangers trading in their seas, and desperate combats often took place between their ships and the "interlopers."

The Eastern seas were rife with pirates, and the company's ships were both well manned and armed to cope not only with them, but with the ships of any state with which we might be at war—an almost chronic condition of affairs tn those days.

When we reflect upon the clumsily built ships of the 17th and early part of the 18th centuries and their ill-cut sails, their imperfect charts and indifferent instruments, the scanty knowledge of the winds and weather to be encountered at the various seasons, the length of time on salt provisions producing the inevitable scurvy, the risks of capture either by pirates or other of the country's enemies, we are moved to admiration at the daring and unconquerable energy of these old-time navigators, and their crews.

Not only were there the known dangers to be apprehended, but the imaginative spirit of those times, conjuredjup a host of other and fearful dangers, which were supposed to beset the mariner in every sea, the great sea serpent, the magnetic rocks, octopi which grappled whole ships, the fatal fire, &c Such were of the perils of the deep.

Their voyages too were of indefinite length, their knowledge of the Trade winds faulty, the supply of water in the casks soon failed, preserved vegetables were unknown as were the marvellous antiscorbutic properties of lime juice.

Labour in those days was cheap and the crews numerous, consequently mechanical purchases did not receive the attention given to them now, and thus improvements were slow. Still the progress of invention was being extended over maritime matters.

Sir Walter Raleigh in 1650 published a book relating to the recent inventions such as the striking of the topmast, &c Steinitz quoting him in his great work on the ship gives:—"together with "the chain pump which takes up twice as much "water as the ordinary did, we had lately added "the bonnet and drabler. To the courses we have. "devised studding sayles, top-gallant sayles, sprit "sayles, top sayles, the weighing of the anchor by "the capstan is also new, &c, &c"

The modern shipowner in these days of telegraphs, ocean mails and railways can scarcely realise the position in which he would have stood in the early days, when after the ships left England, months and sometimes even years passed by without news, either for good or bad, reaching him. The Shipping Chronicles were delightfully vague: In an old chronicle I came across some years ago, an account given of "certyne shyppes sent out to India and China under foreign commission's with English and Irish officers. *Anno* 1715 "St. Francisco Xavier," Mr. Johnson supra cargo sailed from England to Holland, thence to Lisbon, and sailed thence to East Indies with a Portugal commission in September 1715. She traded on the coast of Choromandel, and in Bengal, returning to the Brasiles and thence to Lisbon, are not sure when. *Anno* 1719 "Prince Eugene," called the "Charles Galley," was at Surat, September 1719 thence went to the Malabar coast—It is said the pyrates took her off the Cape of Good Hope returning for Europe. *Anno* 1719-20 "Blackmore," 240 tons, bound for Cadiz and thence to the East Indies. It is credibly reported that she was to take her supra cargoes and some mates at Dover. *Anno* 1719 a large ship from Holland, 500 tons, sailed from Ostend for China about May 1719 (according to report). "Wirtemburg," said to be designed for China—but it is not certain whether she went or not."

Lloyds, however, changed all that, and as trade increased and with it the business of underwriting, &c, thei laws had to be continually improved and added to, to meet the claims of damage, demurrage and other losses incidental to shipping, the questions of compensation for which, became not only more numerous but more intricate and perplexing.

So much space in the ships of commerce up to even the early part of this century, was taken up as gundeck, magazines, crew space, &c, that to overload them with cargo on the outward and frequently on the homeward passage was almost unknown. Still such occasions did happen and when we consider the enormous sums that their cargoes realised at their destinations, we can appreciate the temptation, after the main deck guns had been struck down into the hold and the ports caulked up, to add "just a few more tons" to the venture.

A very notable case in point, which was a matter of enormous expense to the owners, was that of the old "Duke of Grafton", which loaded a cargo of pepper at Bencoolen about the year 1768. The accounts read that she did so take such a quantity of pepper on board much against the opinion of the Governor of Bencoolen and thro' having to stow all her water on deck "was so over"loaded that she became near foundering on her "passage. She became so distressed in bad weather "that the officers and men have insisted to cut "away the masts and heave part of the cargo over"board, the uncommon skill and resolution of the "captain alone preventing this from taking place."

"By labouring she became very leaky and washed "the pepper down into her limbers, which was "brought up on deck in the course of pumping and "baling to the amount of above one hundred tons.

"Above one hundred tons have been thrown on "the owners' hands as damaged. In fine, what by her "tedious passage, having been obliged to bear away Ex. Pamphlet on the E. I, Company, published 1768.

"and what by the damage done to the ship and "cargo, arising from her being thus overloaded, the owners will sustain a loss equal to her whole freight, "all which will effectually prevent her or any other "ship from being thus overloaded in future.

It was many years until the Court of Directors issued instructions to their commanders, relating to the lading of the ships. On the Outward passage, however, there was not the same demand for space as on the Homeward, when most of the ships in peace time caulked up their gun deck ports and striking the guns into the holds, filled up the space with such cargoes as tea, silk, spice and indigo.

An order eventually came into force that no ship of the burthen of 1,400 tons and upwards, be permitted to sail from her port of loading in India at a greater draught than 23 feet 6 inches on an even keek CHAPTER II.

THE HONOURABLE "JOHN COMPANY."

IREAD the other day of freights to India being down to 26/6 a ton for general goods, and 8/6 for coals, while the homeward freights from Bombay were 11/-to 11/6 a ton.

If some byegone proprietors of India stock, who in their day complained of freights from,£25 to,£36 a ton, could be suddenly brought into this age of iron, or rather of steel, and confronted with the present freight report to and from the East, their comments would be entertaining.

In those days the risks of loss were of course great, but the ships tho' moderately expensive to build, lasted a very long time. Towards the close of the last century the expense of building "Indiamen" in England was from *£11* to *£13* a ton.

Clearing a ship, say of 800 tons in the river, cost about *£700,* expenses in India averaged then about,£2,300, wages, &c,,£4,000, Insurance reckoned from the outset at 7 guineas / for a ship of the above mentioned size and quality, while,£400 was considered a not inordinate sum to set aside to satisfy claims for damaged goods.

Nor were wages high, seamen getting but 26/-a month, and putting aside the outward profits, the homeward freights of a ship of say 1,200 tons amounted to about,£20,000, allowing her but 1,100 tons at.£18, and 100 tons surplus freight at.£9.

This last was customary in the service, as on a ship being chartered, she was adjudged by the Directorate to carry an amount of cargo considerably less than her burden, and on this amount the full rate of freight was paid, half rates only on the surplus.

It was the practice of the Company to charter the ships from the owners, who had them built especially for the trade, but as the Company only ran them for about four voyages, holding that then they were no longer fit to carry their cargoes, their value was much reduced, as in no other trade could they be profitably employed, so when they had been superannuated from this service, they were sold to tonnage jobbers who freighted them to Government as ordnance ships, mast ships, &c, while in time of peace their value was so reduced, that their hull and stores are frequently sold out for,£1,400 to,£2,000 sterling.

The position of captain of an "Indiaman" was a most lucrative one, in the early days the command was bought and sold, and from,£2,000 to as much as,£10,000 are known to have been given for the post.

It was his absolute property and he could re-sell it, or if he died, the same right passed to his heirs. Latterly, however, this custom was abolished and compensation given instead. Even then he was allowed on the outward passage up to 56 tons of space free, homewards rather less and by letting his apartments to passengers, his emoluments were much increased; in fact when we read of a subaltern paying,£95, and a general officer.£234 for a passage to India, we may easily concede his profits to have ranged from,£4,000 to,£10,000 a voyage of from fourteen to eighteen months.

In 1793 a charter was formulated by which the trade to India was thrown open to private individuals but in Company's ships. Still the profits on their own ventures and the high freights on the ventures of others were sufficient to permit an enormous income to be realised.

» *Vide* Old Pamphlet, published 1768.

But these halcyon days were coming to an end. In 1802 during the peace, mention was made of East India freights falling to 14 a ton, but the Company allowed these ships *£3* a ton in building and home demurrage at *3d.* (three pence) per ton, per day.

Great and constant was the discontent at the Company's monopolies, but the Proprietors naturally held out steadily against reforms which would tend to diminish their profits.

In 1812 a spirited attempt was made to wring from them some of their privileges, by means of an appeal to merchants and manufacturers towards "repelling the arguments set forth by the East India Company" in favour of their exclusive trade. Mention is made of the reasons why people do not now ship by the East India ships, the high rates of freight being prohibitive.

The Hon'ble Company on their side say that there is no necessity for free trade, that then all the clerks and warehousemen would be thrown out of employment, &c, and that already more Indian manufactures and produce is brought over than she can consume, they also remark on the expense they have been put to in building factories and forts abroad, and warehouses in London,

It met with but qualified success, for in 1824 ships were paid by the East India Company,£22 to 27 a ton for the voyage to and from China.

Such exclusive privileges, however, could not be tolerated in a more enlightened age, and in 1833, in deference to the voice of a nation, their charter, tho' renewed until 1854, was drawn up under conditions which entirely changed its character as the Honourable Company was to cease from trade altogether, and to occupy itself with the Government of its Eastern possessions in conjunction with the Board of Control.

As a governing body the East India Company continued until the Mutiny of 1857, after which its administrative functions were absorbed by the Crown.

The fighting ships, the Indian Navy, to the high skill and unremitting patience of whose officers we owe nearly the whole of the surveys of the Red Sea, Arabian Coast, Persian Gulf, Indian and Burmese Coasts and adjacent islands, and to whom belongs the credit of ridding the Malabar Coast of the pirates which had been the terror of local shipping for centuries, was not disbanded until 1862, and thus closed the maritime connection of the greatest Company the world has ever seen.

CHAPTER III. THE FATE OF OLD "JOHN COMPANY'S" SHIPS. THE building of the largest classes of " Indiamen" had practically ceased for some six or seven years previous to the crash, so that comparatively market, were of the largest size.

The trade was free at last, the fall in freights was so marked, that the shippers began to discount their gains.

A few of the shipowning firms, whose business had previously been the chartering of their ships to the H. E. I. C, now placed their ships on the loading berth on their own account. Several ships were bought in by their Commanders who traded with them themselves, and many were sold in the East to local owners, among the latter being many Parsees and other natives, who placed them in the lucrative "Country trade."

But the majority of the large armed ships, which had been running during the French wars, were not suitable for the altered condition of the Eastern Trade.

Of the sixty-one ships despatched by the Honourable Company to India and China, seasons 1831-32 and 1832-33, no less than nineteen were broken up immediately, and all, with the exception of three, changed hands, many fetching good round sums.

Among others were the "Canning" of 1,326 tons which sold for,£5,700 and was immediately (1834) broken-up, The "Lady Melville" sold in 1832 for,£10,000 was broken up in 1834, 1 were the "London" which fetched,£5,900, "Lowther Cas came then into the tonnage tie" 1,507 tons, and "Marquis Huntley" 1,348 tons, the " Warren Hastings" of 1,068 tons, built in 1811, the " Dunira " 1,326 tons, " Macqueen " of 1,359 tons, built in Rochester 1821, "William Fairlie" 1,313 tons and "Farquharson" of 1,437, which latter realised,£6,000; these all shared the fate of the majority between 1835 and 1836, mostly ships over 1,300 tons, and carrying from 30 to 35 guns.

Of some of those which were considered to be advantageously retained in active employment were the "Buckinghamshire" of 1,369 tons, built in Bombay 1816, and sold in 1834 f *£10,550.* The "Inglis" built in Penang 1811, of 1,321 tons, was bought in for,£9,150, but was wrecked 10 years later.

The " Minerva," built in 1813 in Calcutta, sold for,£9,400, was eventually wrecked about 1850, while the old "Scaleby Castle, "built in Bombay 1798, was bought in by Templer for,£6,900 and re-sold a month later with all her stores on board and ready for sea, for no less than,£13,500. The "Thames " of 1,425 tons, built in London 1819, realised in 1832, upwards of,£10,700, while the materials of the "Waterloo," sold for breaking up purposes, fetched,£7,200 and the " Windsor, " built in London in 1818, commanded in 1834 a price of nearly,£8,000.

And some of the redoubtable old ships remained on Lloyds' books for many years after. The "Bombay," builtin 1809, a shipof a little under 1,300 tons, in 1860 was still owned by Duncan Dunbar. The "Herefordshire," built in 1813, was not erased from the "Register" until 1869. The "Earl of Balcarres," a well-known ship, carrying in her palmy days two complete tiers of guns, found her resting place as a hulk on the West Coast of Africa, while the old "Java," built in Calcutta in 1813, still floats as a coal hulk in Gibraltar.

But the firms which had equipped the ships in the old Company's time, soon passed out of the running. What little do we hear now of "Henry Bonham, of Hyde, F. P. Martin, Larkins, or Murray, or of Jos. Hare, Marjoribanks, Borrodale of Mangles, Oldfield, or Ferguson of Calcutta, of Moffatt, or of John Locke. Sir Robert Wigram's name survived as the firm commenced running a fine fleet on their own account to India. The "London," "True Briton," " Essex, " and "Slains Castle,"—ships from 500 to 700 tons, were of these and registered in their name,—were despatched to India 1835 "d 1836. The "Lady Raffles," "Triumph," "Duke of Buccleugh," "Roxburgh Castle," "Sir Edward Paget," "Carnatic," " Malabar," "WindsorCastle," "Walmer Castle," and others.

Not the Blackwall frigates of the same names of the forties and fifties do

I mean, but their predecessors of the "twenties and thirties," were registered by the traditional Firm of Green, at one time in partnership with Wigram. T. & W. Smith of Newcastle, shipbuilders, entered the lists with their own vessels, which were second to none.

Joseph Somes and Duncan Dunbar also competed, and Tyndall of Scarborough despatched his " Africa," 351 tons, "Symmetry" 382 tons, " Iris" 230 tons, &c, first class ships though of small tonnage and built in Scarborough, and many new firms now came into existence to share in the long-coveted East India trade.

The names even of most of such firms given above were a sufficient guarantee for safety and despatch, both to passengers and shippers, and their frigatebuilt ships were of the highest class, mainly oakbuilt ships, excellently fitted, well found and well kept, well manned and ably commanded.

Their arrivals and departures were matters of public interest. The passenger traffic and the bulk of the trooping service were carried on by these ships. Time was of but little importance, safety being the paramount consideration, the royals were taken in, topsails reefed, and the ships made snug every night.

Had the whole shipowning interest been vested in the hands of such firms as these, and a few others whose ships were scarcely inferior, there would have been but little need of the enforced surveys. But the fact remains that some most scandalous ships were sent to sea at that time. Even the convict ships, which for the time being were under the tutelage of the Government, and might reasonably be supposed to be good ships, were often very far from being so.

Ships when worn out in other trades were taken up for this service,—in fact it would seem as if any thing would do for convicts.

The Government practice for many years being to take the lowest tender, a measure which effectually precluded the best class of ship from competing for the service.

*Apropos* of unseaworthy ships, a tradition exists of a ship putting into Plymouth leaky, the crew refusing to proceed. She was taken up the Cattewater, put on the ground and some cargo discharged. As the tide receded, this "basket" of a vessel almost entirely changed her form. Her bow and stern settled to such an extent that it was confidently expected she would part entirely before the flood tide made. The work of discharging the cargo was rapidly proceeded with, the Captain himself evidently expecting an accident.

There was a succession of loud reports consequent on the excessive strains to which the timbers and planking were being subjected, and by the time of low-water much of the deck and topside planking had succumbed, the wood in the vicinity of the iron bolts being absolutely rotten.

Such a dilapidated fabric would, in these days, have been unhesitatingly condemned, and no question of repair, save that of almost entire rebuilding, entertained.

The cargo, however, was discharged and the ship put into the hands of a repairer. The repair, save the word, was, as might be foreseen, conducted on the lines of strictest economy. A few new futtocks were inserted, if the shifts could be studied, so much the better, otherwise as they were unwilling to undergo the expense of removing too much planking or of lifting the ceiling too far down, many rotten timbers were suffered to remain, and in some cases the timbers were shaved down to enable the repairer the better to place them without removing either planking or ceiling.

No question of continuous shifting was entertained and thus the planks were re-bored.

Her stern, overburdened with the weight of a heavy poop had settled in the space of one tide, no less than one foot in forty-five. Still this farcical '' restoration" was proceeded with, though there seems at no time to have been any suggestion of diagonal ties or riders being introducftd.

On being refloated, to a great extent she recovered her original form, and opportunity was taken to insert some new topside planking and deck planks. Even now, had a few stout ties been worked in, much structural stiffness would have been afforded and maintained, but beyond the futtocks, a few new knees and shelving, and the planking mentioned, nothing was essayed.

Though but-97 feet long, the great mass of timbering which formed her head, comprising bobstay pieces, filling chocks, &c, was cut completely off at the desire of the master.

It weighed upwards of five tons and its removal must considerably have relieved the stem. After a month's delay, during which time not a single floor was laid bare for inspection, the cargo was reloaded, and the ship proceeded on her voyage—there being at that date (1818)—no legal authority to restrain her. Looking back from the present era it is difficult to even give credence to it.

As regards navigation, there is no doubt that in the best ships a greater degree of theoretical knowledge obtained then than at the present day, and this is unquestionably attributable to the elaborate system of tables and formula? which has been gradually introduced, tending so much to simplify the practice and to render unnecessary a close acquaintance with the principles underlying the problems.

Many of the inferior class of vessels, however, were sailed with most culpable recklessness and the masters, though sufficiently skilful seamen, frequently exhibited an ignorance of even the rudiments of navigation almost incredible nowadays.

The Honourable East India Company in their time had conducted their own examinations and the large firms generally instituted an examination of their own, but it was not until the middle of the century that the present compulsory system was established.

Still it was an age of progress, and every decade found the vessels structurally more perfect and being proportionately lighter, were able to carry larger cargoes.

Two influences were at work by 1840, the first was the achievement of applying steam propulsion to the largest class of vessel: the other was the introduction of iron shipbuilding and to some of the initial efforts in these directions, we will now turn our attention.

CHAPTER IV.

THE LAST OF THE OLD EAST INDIAMEN.

SO many years have elapsed since the trade in India was thrown open, and so long is it since the extinction of the Old East India Company's shipowning, chartering, and shipping business, that much interest attaching to their enormous ventures has, of necessity, been lost, and the fate of their ships is now traced with considerable difficulty. On the absolute opening of the trade to untrammelled private enterprise, the ships employed by the Company were either disposed of or broken up, and sixty years might fairly be supposed to have seen the last of these fine old vessels.

On a visit to Gibraltar, however, a few weeks ago, a most strange coal hulk attracted my attention. Her shortness, her low bluff bow, and tumble-down sides, her square stern, and the fact of her being pierced by gun-ports on two decks, all pointed to a bygone date. An accommodation ladder hanging down, I went on board, and the appearance of her upper deck confirmed the impression I had already formed of her from outside.

The waist, from the break of the poop to that of the forecastle, was so short as to seem almost a square. On this upper deck were 12 gun-ports, and in the stanchions on either side of them were still to be seen the heavy iron eyebolts for securing the breeching of the guns. One mast still stood, which, being of teak, might be reasonably assumed to have been the original stick. By the courtesy of her master I was shown all that was visible, her hold, being full of coal, checking all exploration below the main deck. On her forecastle head were still showing her knightheads, a stump of a bowsprit protruded from the bow, and one of the original catheads still remained, the other, I was told, had been shorn off by a passing steamer. Her windlass though antiquated, seemed massive enough to have held the "Great Eastern." We descended then into her main-deck. On this deck she had apparently carried twelve guns, and here, as on the upper deck, the breeching bolts for securing her guns to the side still remained, a silent testimony to the stirring times in which she had been afloat.

That these guns were not for mere display, the old East Indiamen showed in many a bloody fight. Their crews, which were numerous, were frequently and carefully exercised both with great guns and small arms, and in some cases their ships were fitted out with a view to coping, for defensive purposes, with a French frigate; and we doubt not that the crews which had in old days assembled around the guns that frowned through these self-same ports, had been to the full determined to uphold the prestige of the "Warren Hastings," "Streatham," "Ceylon," and others which had held their own against greatly superior odds, until, their decks strewed with dead and dying, their masts tottering or shot away, and their guns dismounted, further resistance being futile, their colours had been hauled down by the survivors.

We found, during our wanderings, the old pair of double steering wheels which formerly had their place, as was the custom in those days, under the break of the poop. Now, in the closing days of this grand old ship, they had been removed from their place and utilised as the wheels of the hand winch. The upper and main deck beams were supported by massive teak stanchions handsomely turned. On emerging from below, we found the present owner, Mr. W. J. Smith, the well-known P. & O. agentThis gentleman, who takes a keen interest in old ships generally, takes an especial interest in this one which came into the hands of his firm some time ago.

A romantic and interesting anecdote was related by him bearing on the building of the ship. According to his informant, a French Naval captain, the ship when built was presented to a British Naval officer under the following circumstances:—A girl of birth and position was carried off by savages, and on the British officer landing a party for her rescue, she was found in the bush safe, but in a perfectly nude condition. Her father was so grateful for her deliverance that he built and equipped the " Java," and gave her to the gallant rescuer of his daughter.

Mr. Smith, on hearing this extraordinary story, gave orders that the figurehead should be dug up from the hold where it had lain for many years under the coal cargo, and it was found to represent a woman, her hands crossed over her breast as if hiding her nakedness. After the days of the Honourable Company's trading fleet were over, the "Java" sailed in private ventures, and though shorn of much of her original magnificence, still, if one may judge from the rates of freight and charter then prevailing, was not an unprofitable speculation.

Freights, however, were steadily declining. In 1843, being owned at this time by Mr. Joseph Somes, we find that she was chartered as a transport at the rate of *1js. nd.* per ton, per month.

She eventually came into the hands of Mr. John Hall, of London in 1856 or 1857, and passed out of the register in 1865.

She was built in Calcutta, of teak, in 1813, and in her palmy days, while the century was young, carried thirty guns. Among her earlier notices was one in Steel's List of 1816, when she was in the service of the Honourable Company, and owned by Paxton and Co. A curious fact which speaks volumes to the-excellence of her scantling, and the skill of her builders happened on her passage out to Gibraltar, laden with coal. She struck on the Pearl Rock, which, as most readers are aware, lies to the southward of Carnero point and about a mile from the shore. She got off, however, and came into Gibraltar Bay. It was the intention to dock her at Cadiz, but the underwriters insisting on her returning home to dock she sailed to England. There, on being docked, she was found to have a large piece or rock sticking in her bottom.

Even at her present age, eighty-three years, her only leak is in the vicinity of this spot, as the planking put in by the repairers has not stood the test of time.

As an almost forgotten hulk she lies now, a link in the chain of progression in the art of shipbuilding— a ship that when built was considered a triumph of skill, a credit alike to designer and builder, but now a floating monument to the palmy days of shipping, and a reminder of the ceaseless changes in the phases of commerce.

CHAPTER V. GREEN'S "BLACKWALL" LINE. AX7"HEN we speak of the old passenger sailing V ships which succeeded the Company's "waggons," the ships of Messrs. Green, Wigram, Smith of Newcastle, or Dunbar, &c, suggest themselves first to our mind. The former firm, so inseparably associated with Blackwall, was the outcome of a great ship-building firm, dating back nearly three hundred years. Some of the early ships of the "Company of Merchant Venturers, trading to the East Indies,"— the "Globe," "Hector," and "Thomas," which sailed for India, under the command of Captain Saris, in 1612, were launched from this yard. For centuries, literally, they built men-o'-war for the Crown, and armed merchant ships for the Honourable East India Company; and on the withdrawal of the monopoly of the latter, embarked on the East India trade on their own account. Their earlier vessels—the "Lady Raffles," "Triumph," "Roxburgh Castle," "Duke of Buccleugh," &c, measured but 500 or 600 tons and were despatched at intervals to Bombay, Madras and Calcutta. The high class of these ships, the great attention paid to their upkeep, and their marked immunity from accident, soon gained them a reputation. From the first, the greatest care was exercised in the selection of their officers, several of whom were late of the Honourable Company's service, and on the abolition of "John Company's" ships, offered themselves for employment under the new *regime;* and later on the system of training their own officers, from midshipman to commander, in their own ships, was instituted.

The tonnage of the vessels gradually increased, in fact a retrospective look at the list of their fleet is almost a history of the trade. The names of their vessels recalled the grand old Company's East Indiamen, whose places they so well filled; the "Carnatic," "Windsor Castle," "Malabar," "Prince of Wales," &c, &c

In the middle of the century they commenced running to the Australian Colonies.

Absolute safety was always the great desideratum aimed at, the question of speed being but a secondary consideration; for unlike some of the flying clippers, sacrificing everything to speed, "driving" to make a passage, the Blackwall frigates snugged down early and for a long time the old practice of taking in the first reef of the topsails every night and striking the royal yards on deck was continued.

Yet the majority of their ships were faultless models, perhaps somewhat "apple cheeked" above water at the bow, and with quarter galleried square sterns, which to modern ideas seem heavy, burdened as they were with a lofty poop; below water their lines were as fine as most clippers. But a certain air of solidity and, if I may say so, of majesty seemed always to attend these ships. Their long poops extending often to the mainmast, and part if not the whole of the 'tween decks given up to passengers, provided great accommodation. There was invariably a long forecastle for the housing of the crew, and usually a deck house between the masts. Thus the upper deck was much contracted, though it generally kept pretty dry, due no doubt to the good conduct of the ships in bad weather and their high freeboard.

In a Parliamentary Report in the "fifties" on the manning of merchant ships, these vessels were quoted as examples of well manned ships. In 1849 the "Alfred," a ship of 1,350 tons, was mentioned as carrying a crew of no less than 90 persons, among whom were 5 mates, 3 boat-swains, 2 carpenters, and 41 seamen.

Personalities are, perhaps, out of place in this book, which merely professes to treat of old ships and old firms; but this chapter would not be complete without an allusion to the liberal and patriotic spirit whichever distinguished this firm. The remarks of Mr. Richard Green to his brother shipowners, on the occasions of the great Free Trade discussions, will never be forgotten, and the practical result of them, the "Challenger," did much to raise the spirits of his *confreres* at that timp.

One could ramble on for hours over the story of these old ships, but so many other interesting old vessels claim our attention, that we must impose a limit, so we will pass on to the ships themselves.

Their names were very frequently duplicated, for instance, there was a "Monarch" built in 1833 and another one in 1844. The latter was a magnificent ship of 1,415 tons, she was sold out of their service to Mr. Macey, I believe about 1866, and later on passed into the hands of Mr. W. Savill; afterwards Mr. R. W. Morris of London became the owner, and she was eventually (1876) posted as "Missing" on a voyage from Bombay to Rangoon.

There was a "Roxburgh Castle" built in 1825 of 600 tons, and sold about 1839, and in 1852 they had another "Roxburgh Castle" built to their order in Sunderland. She sailed for a long time in the Australian trade, and contributed doubtless her share to the prosperity of the fleet; on one occasion in 1854 she brought home gold to the amount of,£287,528. She was afterwards sold to the Danes, and was eventually wrecked on the Goodwin Sands in 1876.

The earlier "Malabar" was built in 1834 and measured 647 tons; the second "Malabar," built in 1860, measured 1,219. She was eventually sold out of their service.

The earlier ' Windsor Castle" was built in 1835. of 676 tons measurement. Her reproduction was built in 1857 by Messrs. Pile, of Sunderland. She measured 1,075 tons, and was sold out of their service about 1883. She foundered the following year about 40 miles South of Algoa Bay.

The earlier "Walmer Castle" of 656 tons was built in 1836; the second " Walmer Castle " in 1855. She also, like the " Windsor Castle," was a Sunderland built ship. Like most of these vessels, she was sold and eventually, when owned by Messrs. Welch, was burnt in Samarang when loading sugar for Holland, 1876.

The "Wellesley," built in 1844, 963 tons, was sold to a well-known Indian shipowner, Vallee Gooloo" of Calcutta, about 1874, and became a "country ship." The "Alfred," we have already alluded to. The "Prince of Wales," built in 1842, was one of their largest ships, she was sold out of their service about 1864.

The " Sutlej," built in 1847 was, unfortunately, burnt in Calcutta in 1859. She was one of the very few vessels lost while in their own service.

The "Nile," built in 1858, 1,126 tons, was sold about 1871 and still floats as a coal hulk at Gibraltar, one of the most interesting hulks afloat. I went on board her not very long ago (1896).

The " Blackwall,"a little ship of 674 tons, was sold about 1870 to Mr. Stewart, who ran her for a long time. She was eventually (1884,) wrecked on the shores of Morecambe Bay, on a voyage, St. Johns to Fleetwood, laden with deals.

-The little "Resolute" was lost in 1856. The "Challenger " and her exploits figure in a subsequent chapter on the China clippers.

Then there were two American built ships associated with their firm,—the " Result, " built in Boston in 1853,1,465 tons, and the "Swiftsure," built at the same place in 1854. The latter was sold to Messrs. Hall Brothers, and was eventually (1884)wrecked in Tripoli Harbour.

The " Alwick Castle," built in Sunderland in 1854, 1,087 tons, was sold about 1873 to Mr. Bagshot, and re-sold to Mr. Swyny; afterwards she became the property of Sir John Arnott of Cork, and was wrecked on the Mexico coast when on a voyage—Rotterdam to Manzanillas in 1881.

The "Clarence," built in 1858, 1,104 tons, ld put of-their service about 1873.

The " Dover Castle," built in the same year, 1,002 tons, was sold to Messrs. Shaw, Savill & Co., and re-sold about 1882 to Mr. C. F. Boe of Arendal and re-named " Kem."

The "Newcastle," built in 1859, 1,137tons, sold out of their service about 1877 to Mr. Folly. She was afterwards re-sold to Messrs. Burns, Philip and Company, and it was at last decided to convert her into a hulk for their transhipment business in Thursday Island, Queensland. On her journey up the Queensland coast, while threading her way among the intricate reefs and shoals there, she was wrecked on Bushy Island Reef.

The "Lady Melville," built in the same year, 966 tons, ran through many changes of ownership, and port of registry. After being a "Country-ship" for some years, she was sold to the Norwegians and re-named "Anna."

The " Renown " was sold about 1881 to Bollard pf Bremen

Thc " Highflier," another familiar name in connection with East India Shipping, was built in 1861, and afterwards passed into the hands of Ramien of Elsfleth and so out of ken.

The "Shannon," built the following year, 1,272 tons, was sold after more than 20 years' service, and some time afterwards became the property of Mr. J. C. Ellis of Sydney, and eventually, 1888, on a voyage—Newcastle (New South Wales) to Wilmington, was condemned in the South Pacific, bein leaky.

The " Lord Warden," built in the same year as the "Shannon," measured 1,23710ns. She was eventually sold to Ossoinak of Fiume.

The "Childers," 1,016 tons, built in 1863, came to grief in the China Seas.

The "Superb," an iron ship, well meriting her name, was built in 1866. She was sold, and not long ago I saw her in Rangoon, but her great ports were closed up, the accommodation being confined to a small space aft.

There was also the "Carlisle Castle," an iron ship built in 1868, measuring 1,458 tons. She too was sold out of their service.

There were other fine old frigate-built wooden ships, I have but mentioned those the best known.

Early in the "seventies" Messrs. Green inaugurated a steamship service and built two steamers,—the *f.* Viceroy" of 1,864 tons and 240. H.P., and the "Sultan" of about the same size and horse-power But these vessels did not meet with the success which had attended the old Blackwall sailing ships, and they were sold.

The " Viceroy " eventually foundered in the North Atlantic on a voyage, New Orleans to Bremen, 1884; while the "Sultan," sold to the Spaniards, was renamed and is now the " Asia" of Cadiz.

In 1875 they built another magnificent iron sailing ship, the "Melbourne," and she is still (1896) a favourite passenger vessel, running to the Australian Colonies under the name of " Macquarie."

Mr. Richard Green died comparatively early, being but 58 years old at the time of his death. Such men are few; the efficiency and credit of his ships, and the comfort of the crews were to him far more than any enhancement of his profits by the "cutting down" the upkeep, wages and food. From 1834 t' of his death in 1863, a period of nearly thirty years, as has been shewn, but four ships were lost, *viz.,* the " Conqueror," " City of Poonah," "Madagascar," and "Sutlej." His charities were proverbial, and the conditions of his will were as indicative of his generous and kindly nature, as were the munificent gifts and endowments bestowed during his lifetime. His "Home"—"Green's Home for Seamen"—was carried on for about 10 years after his death, when it was closed in accordance with a legal decision, though much against the wishes of the Messrs. Green.

The old name is still a familiar advertisement in the shipping columns of almost every newspaper, but though the altered conditions of trade, consequent on the great development of the steamship, have closed the career of the old "Blackwall frigates," their glorious prestige will last as long as sailing ships exist.

## CHAPTER VI.

T. AND W. SMITH OF NEWCASTLE, TXTELL in the foremost rank of the great sailing shipowners, must be placed the historic Firm of T. and W. Smith of Newcastle;, and for an account of their early history, I take the liberty of quoting copiously from a very interesting article which appeared in the *Newcastle Weekly Chronicle Supplement* some time back.

"Thomas Smith, eldest son of the Alderman, was born at St. Lawrence, November 27th, 1783; William, his brother, was born at the same place on the 15th July 1787. Thomas served with his father as ropemaker; William was apprenticed to Mr. Row, shipbuilder at St. Peter's.

"Mr. Row carried on an extensive business, and attained the distinction of building the largest ships that up to his time had been launched into the waters of the Tyne.

"Local annalists record with pride the ease and grace with which, on the 3rd of November 1808 "His Majesty's ship "Bucephalus" 970 tons measurement, rated at 32, but pierced for 52 guns " glided from the ways at Mr. Row's Yard, followed a fortnight later by a very handsome small ship of war called the "Woodlark." William Smith was just out of his time when the "Bucephalus" floated away from St. Peter's. Within a couple of years later, he and his father and brother had acquired Mr. Row's interest in St. Peter's Dock, and formed themselves into a firm of shipbuilders under the title of William Smith and Company. Thus by the end of the year 1810 the business of the Smiths was expanded into two firms— Thomas Smith, roper, St. Lawrence, and William Smith and Co. shipbuilders, St. Peter's—with a joint office in the Broad Chare, Newcastle.

'' For a time the vessels constructed by the new firm at St. Peter's were of the ordinary type, but in 1828 having meanwhile extended their operations by the acquisition of a graving dock at North Shields, they began to build ships for the East India Trade. Before long they had formed a line of passenger vessels which ran under their management between London, the Capeof Good Hope, Madras and Calcutta; and successfully competed with that of the Blackwall shipowners, Messrs. Green & Wigram.

"For many years these two firms held possession of the East India passenger trade.

"Under their respective flags, the development of the wooden sailing ship was carried to a high degree of perfection. Commanded by officers whose names were "household words" in maritime commerce, Smith's East India liners and the competing vessels of Green & Wigram became in point of speed, form and equipment, the admiration of naval men and the pride of the mercantile community.

"The first East Indiaman built at St. Peter's was the " Duke of Roxburgh," a ship of 417 tons.

"From the date of her construction the firm went on increasing the size and excellence of their vessels, until in 1846-48 they reached the highest point in the "Marlborough," 1,387 tons and the "Blenheim," 1,392 tons. These two ships were submitted to a special Government survey, and reported as frigates fit for carrying armaments. Thenceforward the size of the East Indiamen declined, and the last of them, the "St. Lawrence," was of the measurement of 1,188 tons. Besides these great merchant ships, Messrs. Smith turned out of their yard at St. Peter's, several war vessels, notably the "Carlo Alberto" in 1852-53, and eleven gunboats for the Government during the Crimean war.

"It was in 1814, four years after taking over the business of Mr. Row, that Messrs. W. Smith & Co, extended their operations to North Shields.

"They obtained a lease of Laing's Dock at that place, acquired a quay for the deposit of ballast —forming in time the huge mound near Cable Den, on which the Shields' time-gun stands, opened a raff yard and began the building and repairing of ships at St. Peter's.

"Eventually Laing's Dock became too small for their operations, and in 1850, upon land adjoining, they opened a new one of their own construction, then much the largest in the river. A couple of years later they commenced iron shipbuilding there with ten lighters for the Viceroy of Egypt. The first steamship built by the firm (launched at North Shields in 1854) was the "Zingari" for Mr. Ralph Ward Jackson of West Hartlepool—a vessel which at the good old age of thirty-seven years still performs a regular service between the Tyne and the Continent. Their third steamer, the " Chasseur," was bought by Government for service in the Crimea.

"Fitted up as a floating factory with engineering shop, foundry, saw-mill, &c, and a full complement of artisans, she was sent direct from the shipyard to Balaclava, and became a useful auxiliary to our army at Sebastopol. This vessel, also, is still afloat, employed in Government work among the fleet at Sheerness.

"Upon the death of Alderman Smith in 1836, the firm changed its name to that of " Thomas & William Smith " and by that title it has ever since been known. Under the management of the two brothers it acquired fame and fortune. Besides the East Indiamen, the firm owned a fleet of colliers that ran between the Tyne and the Thames, and in connection with that and their other maritime undertakings, they had coal hulks at Gravesend, a sail-making loft at Blackwall, and a warehouse at the East India Docks. They also established themselves as shipowners and brokers in London, and carried on an extensive business in the sailing and chartering of ships there; while upon the Tyne, the shipyards and ropery were employed to the fullest extent of their resources.

"The personal history of the two brothers, by whose energy and foresight the Firm of T. & W. Smith was raised to the highest rank among the great commercial houses of the kingdom, presents few features of public interest. Strictly men of business, they found their time fully absorbed in the ever widening circle of industrial progress, and rarely stepped beyond it.

"The elder brother, as we have seen, occupied the post of a Sheriff during his father's second Mayoralty; the younger brother filled the same office in 1830.

"With these appointments, their participation in public life began and ended.

"At the sale of the Brandling estates

in 1852, High Gosforth House and 2,100 acres of land were purchased by Mr. Thomas Smith for,£71,260.

"He had occupied the mansion for several years previously and there he continued to reside until his death on the 29th of April 1856. United late in life to Margaret Collingwood, daughter of Mr. Percival Fenwick, he left no issue, and the property and business passed into the hands of his brother. Mr. William Smith removed from Benton Lodge to Gosforth House soon after his brother's decease, and died thereon the 13th of October 1860, leaving, by his marriage with Margaret, daughter of Major Werge, a son—Mr. Thomas Eustace Smith, sometime M. P. for the borough of Tynemouth.

"After both brothers had passed away, the operations of the firm were Carried on for several years by Mr. Thomas Eustace Smith, and two partners. One of the partners, Mr. James Southern, managed the London department, while the works upon Tyneside were conducted by the other partner, Mr. George Luckley. It may be interesting to state in conclusion that the historical Firm of T. & W. Smith still flourishes under the management of Alderman Smith's great-grandson, Mr. Eustace Smith the younger."

Thus runs the article 1—

Their ships in many respects resembled men-o'war, their build and general equipment being almost identical, the larger class with frigates, the smaller with the corvettes.

f

Their moulding, scantling and finish were equal to that prevailing in the highest type of war vessel; nor were even the ports in the side wanting, and so at short notice they could have been completed entirely as men-o'«war.

The grandest of all their ships were undoubtedly the "Marlborough" and the "Blenheim;" the former, which eventually became a coal hulk in Gibraltar, was broken up but a few years ago,—about 1888, I think. Other well-known ships were the " Gloriana," 1,057 tons, built in 1843; the " Bucephalus," 985 tons, built 1840; the "Hotspur," 1,142 tons, built 1851, which was eventually wrecked at Madras, 1872; and the " St. Lawrence," 1,094 tons, built 1861. The latter was one of the last frigate-built vessels launched, s

I saw her in Sydney, N. S. W., about 1882, having brought there a cargo of lumber from Puget Sound, —a grand old ship with a low bow, square stern and overhanging quarter galleries, and with a very long poop. In her palmy days, judging by the old passenger lists, her great accommodation was often fully taken up; but in her declining days, when under another flag, she was run on less liberal lines, most of her sumptuously apparelled cabins had been stripped and turned into store rooms, lockers, &c, the great ports closed up, and hardly a vestige remained to remind one of former greatness and prosperity.

Thus it has been with all the "old timers "; and the time must assuredly come when the present crack P. & O. and Orient liners will be looked upon with something like contempt, by a future generation, as antiquated and slow. But the names of the modern liners will never linger in the memory of those connected with the sea, as the well known names of the old frigate-built ships have done, whose annual or biennial voyages were matters of such widespread interest.

CHAPTER VII. SOME NOTES ON EARLY STEAM NAVIGATION. THIS Chapter should be a short one, as a dissertation on early Steam Navigation scarcely comes within the province of this book; its history, even of the initial stages, has been so exhaustively dealt with in excellent works, devoted especially to that subject, that I propose to confine myself merely to a retrospect—an outline as it were, and then to pass on to the eventual fates of some of the more important pioneer vessels in the annals of Steam Navigation.

The initial stages referred to above, really date back to 1543, the time when Blasco de Gary, a Spaniard of an ingenious turn of mind, applied steam power to propel a vessel. The efforts of Denis Papin in 1647; of Jonathan Hulls in 1737; of the Marquis of Jouffroy in 1751; of Fitch in 1785; of Rumsey the following year, and Symington in 1788, all marked progressive steps.

But it was not until 1819 that an Ocean passage was actually attempted. This pioneer ocean steamer, the "Savannah," a vessel of 300 tons burden, built in New York, left Savannah for Liverpool April 10th, amid much enthusiasm. Her paddle wheels were so arranged that when she was required to proceed under sail only, they could easily be disconnected and lifted on deck. Under the command of Captain Rogers she made the passage in 22 days, having been under sail only but seven days. She afterwards went to Russia, where the Czar honoured her with a visit and presented the Captain with a pair of iron chairs. At that time coal was not in general use as fuel for either land or sea engines, and wood was used exclusively in the "Savannah." The results, commercially considered, were neither sufficiently promising to justify an extension of the service, nor even a repetition of the experiment, so she reverted to a sailing ship and afterwards ran regularly between New York and Savannah; and it was while on one of these voyages that she was ultimately wrecked on Long Island, New York.

The next important advance was the little "Enterprise." In 1824 the residents of Bengal, by a public subscription, offered a bonus of 8,000 to the first vessel that should steam out within a stipulated time. The "Enterprise," which had been built at Messrs. Gordon & Company's yard, Deptford, the previous year, left Falmouth, August 16th,-1825, for Calcutta, with a view to competing for the bonus. She measured 470 tons, was 122 feet long on her keel, 27 feet beam and barque rigged. Her appearance was somewhat extraordinary, the funnel being as high as the foretop, and she had that cumbrous apple bow, common to all ships of that date. Her boiler, we are told, was of copper and weighed 32 tons, costing *£700.* At full speed in fine weather and burning from 10 to 12 tons of coal daily, she made 6 to 7 knots per hour. She arrived at Diamond Harbour, December 8th, after a passage of 113 days and some odd hours, made up as follows:—

D. H.

... 2 18 ... 7 21 ... 62 23 ... 40 3 113 17

As the voyage was not effected within the required time, half the bonus was paid to the Commander and

At St. Thomas'

„ Cape

Under Steam

Sail

the vessel purchased by the Government. An excellent account of the transactions appeared in Mr. Prinsep's Parliamentary Report.

She was soon followed out to the East by another vessel, the "Falcon," which had originally been Lord Yarborough's Yacht (" Falcon No. I," I think). A London firm had bought this vessel—a barque of 170 tons—to despatch to Calcutta, purely as a commercial venture, the owners, we are told in Prinsep's report, owing to the Burmese War, anticipating a demand for such a vessel. She sailed out, not using her two 24 horse-power engines at all on the passage. The price demanded for her is described as being excessive and defeated the aim of the projectors of the scheme, and while they were still endeavouring to negotiate her sale, peace was proclaimed, so that the opportunity of selltng her to the Government was lost. The coasting trade of India then was not developed, and as the trade between India and China was carried on entirely in sailing vessels, and no other employment presenting itself to a steamer pure and simple, her engines were removed, she was registered at Calcutta and put into the opium trade, and we are told she "was one of the fastest and prettiest opium clippers belonging to the port."

The Hudson's Bay Company's steamer "Beaver" claims more than a passing notice. An account of her loss, somewhat poetically written, appeared in the *Scientific American* not long ago, and was reproduced in the *Steamship.* As some readers may not have seen the account, I reproduce it here:—

"Nearly sixty years have passed since the Hudson's Bay Company's steamer "Beaver" floated down the Thames. She was the pioneer of the Pacific Ocean and was the first European steamer to round Cape Horn, her passage from London to Astoria, Oregon, consuming 163 days. She was 101 feet by 20 feet by n£ feet; tonnage 109J. The two engines of 35 horse-power each were built by Boulter and Watt, Birmingham; cost. £4,500 and weighed 52 tons. She was built of oak, and copper fastened, and was used as a fur trading vessel, and on one of these trips, coal was discovered on Vancouver Island. In 1849, during the gold excitement, many miners took passage on the little steamer. When steaming out of Burrard Inlet in 1888 she struck on a rock, and wrapped in a sheet of troubled waters, and with head resting on a huge barnacle-clad boulder, the Pacific pioneer passed into history. Unsuccessful attempts were made to float her, and she remained on the rocks for nearly four years. An attempt was made to take her to the World's fair, but was abandoned owing to her damaged condition and cost of transportation. Messrs. McCain and Menzies of Vancouver, purchased the vessel and are making up 975 lbs. of old brass and copper, into souvenir medals; the timber has been worked up into souvenir canes, i&c"

By the time this little steamer of the Far North had begun to ply, the Peninsula Company, afterwards the P. & O. , was in full swing, and soon after the Cunard line commenced running with the "Britannia," "Arcadia," " Caledonia" and "Columbia," and also the Royal Mail Steam Packet Company. The career of these three great companies is historical, and as they are still flourishing and likely to be so, I trust, for many generations to come, they will not be dealt with in this work.

The Navy too had recognised the importance of this invention, and the H.E. I.C. had, ere this, several war steamers in Eastern waters.

In 1834 a select committee of the House of Commons, which was convened to enquire into, and report upon, the subject of mail communication by steam between England and India, declared—"That steam navigation between Bombay and Suez having on five successive seasons been brought to the test of experiment, it was expedient that measures be immediately taken for the regular establishment of steam communication with India by the Red Sea, the expense of the establishment to be shared equally by the East India Company and His Majesty's Government; that the communication with India by the Persian Gulf and Euphrates was not brought to the test of experiment, and that it was desirable that it should be brought to such a test and that a grant of 20,000 be made by Parliament for that purpose."

In 1839, The East India Steam Navigation Company was projected, and to this disastrous undertaking, I have devoted a special chapter.

Referring again to the old Atlantic companies. In 1833 the " Royal William," a steamer of about 500 tons, built in Quebec by Mr. James Grondie in 1831, and owned by the Incorporated Quebec and Halifax Steam Navigation Company, crossed over in 21 days. She had formerly been trading between Quebec, Montreal and Halifax, and must not be confounded with the later "Royal William," a British built vessel owned by the City of Dublin Steam Packet Company. I mention this here, because some accounts are so delightfully vague on the subject of the two early Transatlantic steamers bearing the same name. Returning, however, to No. 1, she made but one voyage and was then sold to the Portuguese Government. She had a curious career, and eventually became a coal hulk, and a few years ago changed hands for *£11.*

In 1839 the " Sirius," "British Queen," and "President," owned by the British and North American Company, commenced running. The "Sirius" measured but 700 tons. She was engined by Thomas Wingate of Glasgow, and after a short career was taken off the line to run between Dublin and Cork, and in 1847, while in this service, was wrecked in Ballycotton Bay with the loss of many lives.

Contemporary with her was the steamer "Great Western," the outcome of a Bristol venture. She was designed by Isambard K. Brunei, and as the subscribed capital of the projectors reached,£250,000, to cover the cost of but two steamers, no expense was spared in her construction and equipment. The intention of the Great Western Steamship Company, as the undertaking designated itself, was to build two steamers of 1,20O tons and 300 horse-power to run between Bristol and New York. The share capital, as stated above, was divided into 2,500 shares of,£100 each and,£63,000 was expended on the "Great Western." She left Bristol, April 8th, 1838, for New York, arriving April 23rd. Mr. Patterson of Bristol built this vessel, she was 212 feet long by 35 feet 4 inches beam by 23 feet 2 inches deep, and measured 1,340 tons. Shortly afterwards the "Great Britain," an iron ship also by Patterson of Bristol, was placed on the line amid much *iclat,* my father being among the vast throng of spectators who witnessed her launch. She measured 1,750 tons, was of 500 horse-power and cost upwards of,£120,000. Originally she had five masts, but latterly her rig was altered to that of a three-masted ship, and the excellence of her lines was afterwards proved by her passages as a sailing ship. This ship, launched in 1843, is yet afloat as a hulk, and her eventful history will be found in a subsequent chapter:—that of the Auxiliary steamers.

Returning to the "British Queen" and the "President;" the former, a ship of 2,016 tons and 500 horse-power, 275 feet by 60 feet by 27 feet, made the passage in 13 daysj 18 hours and some odd minutes, but being too expensive to run, was sold to the Belgian Government in 1841. The " President," a sister ship, after three voyages, left New York for Liverpool, was known two days later to have encountered a terrific storm, and was never heard of again. This disaster terminated the existence of the Company.

The Great Western Company struggled on, the "Great Western" Herself making twenty-two voyages in four years, on one occasion making the passage in 13 days, 6 hours, and some odd minutes. But they received no Aid from Government, in spite of the great benefits which had accrued to the country from this spirited enterprise. The total cost of maintaining the vessel per mile was declared to be 2330 shillings, while the gross receipts reached but 2250 shillings. In 1846 the "Great Britain," one of the strongest ships ever built, was wrecked in Dundrum Bay while on her passage to New York, and the Company could not stand up against a misfortune of such magnitude. The following year the " Great Western" was sold to the Royal Ma1l Steam Packet Company, and while there, was a successful ship under the altered conditions. But such strides were being taken in steam navigation, that she soon became obsolete and in 1857 was broken up. In 1847 thc " Grcat Britain" was raised, and eventually acquired by the Liverpool and Australian Steam Navigation Company, in whose service we shall hear again of this interesting vessel.

The "Royal William" and "Liverpool," owned by the Transatlantic Company of Liverpool, followed quickly in the steps of the "Sirius" and ''Great Western;" the former, which, strictly speaking, was the "Royal William" No. 2, was chartered from the City of Dublin Steam Packet Company. She was built by Messrs. Wilson of Liverpool and engined by Preston and Faucett, measured 817 tons, was 175 feet long, 27 feet beam and *174* feet depth, and made the passage out in 19 days and home in 14. The " Liverpool," a ship of 1,311 tons and 464 horsepower, made six voyages; one passage being performed in eleven days and eighteen hours, and was sold to the P. & O. Company, who changed her name to the " Great Liverpool." She was wrecked eventually off Finisterre in 1846.

By this time the Cunard Company had established a firm hold upon the trade, and shortly after a French line was started; four ships ran, but it proved unprofitable and was given up. A Belgian line followed, but met with the same fate.

Then the Americans organised a line of steamers to run from New York to Bremen, calling at Southampton and placed the two steamers "Washington" and "Hermann" on this service. The former sailed from New York, June 1847. She was received at Bremen with great rejoicings. Indeed, enthusiasm ran to such a pitch that it seemed as if sufficient honour could not be paid to the new arrival. It was early discovered, however, that American steamers could not compete in point of economical working with British-built and owned steamers and at last, in 1858, they were taken off the line and sold in New York, realising but $45,000.

The Collins line commenced running in 1850; the Americans were, as may be imagined, on their mettle when they perceived how successful were the operations of the Cunard, both in extending their business and realising dividends, &c In order to compete again for a share of the Transatlantic trade, theybuilt four steamers, the "Atlantic," "Arctic," "Baltic, "and "Pacific" and placed them on the service, under the guidance of Mr. Collins, managing owner of a successful line of Transatlantic sailing packets. The ' Collins" steamers were built of wood, mainly of oak, and neither pains nor expense were spared in their construction, and as they first floated into their element, the citizens of the United States might well have felt proud of their handiwork. The subsidy conceded by the United States Government was upwards of 178,750 per annum, for which a high rate of speed was demanded, the best passage being made by the "Arctic," *viz.,* 9 days, 17 hours and 12 minutes.

It was, however, doomed to misfortune: for, while the service was being carried on at enormous expense and with most unremunerative returns, their steamer "Arctic" was run into, and sunk by the French steamer "Vesta," near Cape Race in 1854, and 219 passengers were lost and many of the crew. Again in 1856 they had the misfortune to lose the "Pacific," which left Liverpool for New York, January 23rd, with 45 passengers and a crew of 141, and was never heard of again. For weeks afterwards a most diligent look-out was observed by other Transatlantic vessels for boats or even some of her wreckage, and two Government steamers, the " Tartar " and the " Desperate," made a prolonged, though unsuccessful, search for the missing liner, but absolutely no trace of her was ever afterwards seen. The "Adriatic" now appeared on the scene, for long spoken as the "monster ship;" like the others she was a wooden paddle steamer with a straight stem and barque rigged. She was larger, however, measuring 354 feet 8 inches long by 50 feet beam and 33 feet 1 inch depth; her principal anchors weighed 3 tons, she had two funnels and carried a large crew, 53 on deck, 76 in the engine room and 54 in the saloon, 183 in all. But the losses incurred by the foundering of the two steamers and the ruinous competition then prevailing, proved too much for the Company, and in 1858 they woundup. The steamers were sold and a year or two afterwards saw them running between New York and Aspinwall. The "Adriatic" soon afterwards came into the possession of the English, and lay for many years at Southampton.

Another early firm was the Clyde Screw Steam Packet Company when Mr. Murray adventured the steamship "Clyde "on the New York and Glasgow line in the early fifties. She was a steamer of 1,169 and 250 horse-power, and was commanded by Captain Henderson of Anchor Line renown.

I don't propose in this Chapter to go much further ahead with the Atlantic Companies because, chronologically, we so soon come to those nourishing now; but among others in the fifties I will mention the Glasgow and New York Steam Navigation Company, whose service was maintained by the "Edinburgh," "New York," and "Glasgow;" the Montreal Ocean Steam Navigation Company, now the Allan Line; the Inman Line; the American— Havre Line; the Belgian Line; and the Vanderbilt Line. In this latter undertaking Mr. Vanderbilt was represented as standing alone, receiving no subsidy for maintaining the line between New York, Southampton and Havre in competition with other lines, some of which were subventioned to the extent of 12,500 to 19,750 dollars per voyage. The first vessel across was the "Vanderbilt, followed by the "Ariel," and "North Star."

In 1858 the Galway Line, or rather I should say the first Galway Line, commenced. The idea uppermost in the minds of the projectors was, of course, the shortening of the long ocean passage; but the great expense of conveying passengers and goods to and from Galway did not sufficiently compensate for the shorter sea voyage. The pioneer steamer on the line to New York was the " Indian Empire," followed by the "American Empire," but for reasons already stated, the scheme was unsuccessful. The Company too forfeited their subsidy through an unfortunate breach of faith.

The second scheme was devised with the object of organising a fast steamship service between Galway and St. John's, Newfoundland; a detailed history of this unfortunate enterprise is to be found in Lindsay's invaluable work, volume IV, and also in the Parliamentary Report on the proceedings of the Company 1863. It was projected—Mr. Lindsay tells us—by some English and Irish gentlemen, most of whom had little knowledge, and certainly no experience, of the business they were about to undertake. They offered to land the mails (from Galway) in St. John s in the unprecedented time of six days, and to convey them thence to New York for a subvention of 3,000 a voyage. I append a time-table of the Royal Atlantic Steam Navigation Company:—

From Galway to America and *vice versa*—,,, Galway to New York April to D. Htm.

October (inclusive) 11 2 ,, Galway to Boston during like months 11 16 ,, New York to Galway do.... 10 o

,, Boston to do. do.... 10 4

,, Galway to New York Nov. to

March inclusive 13 o ,, Galway to Boston do.... 13 12 ,, New York to Galway do.... 10 10,, Boston to do. do... . 1r 2 The account further tells us that four vessels were contracted for, to be of the highest class and conforming to all the requirements of the Admiralty, with whom specifications had been lodged for approval. Two were ordered of Messrs. Palmer of Newcastle, *viz.* :— the "Connaught" and "Hibernia," at a cost of,£95,000 each, and two of Messrs. Samuelson of Hull, the "Anglia" and the "Columbia," costing,£97,750 each. They were to accomplish twenty statute miles an hour in smooth water, a stipulation which was not fulfilled as the "Connaught ' on her trial trip realised but 13 knots.

They seemed to be predestined to failure: for, owing to various causes, the ships were not delivered at the stipulated time, necessitating the chartering of another steamer, the "Parana," with which to commence the service. She left Galway on the 27th June i860 and arrived at St. John's in.7 days 13 hours, and in New York 11 days 17 hours from her departure: 15 hours behind her contract time. The " Connaught," the succeeding steamer, delivered her mails in Boston 22 hours late, and on her second voyage was burnt. The "Hibernia," on her way round from the builders, was so damaged in a gale that she never entered the service at all. The "Columbia" was severely damaged by ice the same year.

To supply the place of the "Connaught".. and "Hibernia, " the Company purchased the steamer "Adriatic" late of the Collins line, and chartered the "Prince Albert," a steamer of 1,700 tons gross and 400 horse-power, built in Antwerp, in 1856; but the great disasters, succeeding each other so quickly, had exhausted both their resources and credit, and in May 1861, Mr. Lindsay tells us, they terminated their contract.

In 1863 the contract was renewed and the service again attempted with two chartered ships, late of the General Screw Line, and the "Anglia "(the latter being wrecked the same year); but met with no better success than had attended the two previous undertakings... ..-..

Long ere the Pacific had been exploited and in the "forties," the Pacific Steam Navigation Company commenced operations on the coast of South America With some handsome little brig-rigged steamers. To the Brazils several firms had started. In addition to those now flourishing was the South American and General Steam Navigation Company. They purposed maintaining the line to the River Plate *via* Lisbon, &c, with the " Bahiana," " Brazillira," " Lusitania," and "Olinda," while the "La Plato" connected with Rio Janiero, and in 1854 some reasonable hopes existed.

. The Mediterranean lines were well served by Mr, Mongredian of Liverpool, later by Messrs. McKean, McLarty and Lamont, the present firm of Papayanni; the P. & O.; Messrs. Jones & Chappie; the Moss Line, &c, &c A very interesting steamer ran in the service of the latter firm—the "Luxor," an auxiliary vessel of 1,140 tons and 120 horsepower, formerly the "Hope," one of the old West African Mail steamers. Also by several foreign lines, the Austrian Lloyds, Messageries Maritimes, &c

Out to the East Indies, the steam frigates of the Honourable Company, which for so many years had carried the mails between Suez and Bombay, had given place to the steamers of the P. & O. The East India Steam Navigation Company, after a brief existence, had succumbed to fate. Later on the P. & O. extended their services to Galle, Madras, and Calcutta. The General Screw Steamship Company, which had started so full of hope, had come lamentably to grief, and in 1856 they were succeeded in their Calcutta contract by the auxiliary steamers of Mr. W. S. Lindsay of Tynemouth, a shipowner of much experience. He undertook it with seven vessels for,£41,000, but it was not successful, and the contract was abandoned in twelve months. The steamers were put into other trades or sold, and so another steam line, full of promise, was closed.

The "England," a steamer of 949 tons and 100 horse-power, was built at Port Glasgow in 1856. She was the first vessel to sail on the line, and the freight and passage-money earned on her first trip augured more favourably than future results justified. She was sold to the Japanese in 1861 and sunk at the bombardment of Kagosima in 1863. The "Scotland " afterwards pioneered a line under the American flag between San Francisco and China.

The China coasting trade had been opened up. On the Indian Coast, besides the opium traders, were a few private steamers of small size; the Bombay Steam Navigation Company established in 1845, and later on, the Calcutta and Burmah Steam Navigation Company, which, from a small beginning, developed into the British India Steam Navigation Company, through the marvellous energy and prescience of Mr. (afterwards Sir) William Mackinnon. A very interesting article bearing on the foundation of the undertaking appeared in the *Times of India,* being an extract from Martineau's "Life of Sir Bartle Frere."

Until late in the "seventies " there were some weirdlooking steamers, both in Eastern and Far Eastern waters. On the Australian coast, too, some extraordinary vessels cruised about from port to port, both paddlersand screw. A very interesting steamer the "You Yangs" was lost quite lately near Willoughby. She had three masts and her engines were aft, while she had that flat heavy "Scott-Russell" type of stern, now no longer to be met with. She did good service during the Crimean war. Local and River steam navigation had also been making great progress; the General Steam Navigation Company, which claims to date from 1824, being, I believe, the oldest firm. One frequently sees prints of some of their earlier vessels; little brig-rigged paddle-wheel steamers, the funnel bell-mouthed, towering above the fore and main tops, the captain on the bridge connecting the paddle-boxes, energetically waving an enormous telescope, while passengers in preVictorian costumes were grouped about the decks.

Before closing this chapter, a reference to some early American steamers will be interesting. They had not been idle over there, for, in the " forties," their rivers and lakes swarmed with steam-boats. An account of some of their pioneer vessels, and of the industrial conditions under which they were built and worked, is to be found in the *Progress of America.*

A writer in the *Western Monthly Magazine* of that date tells us that the first "steamboat built in Western waters, was built in Pittsburg in 1811, under the name of "Orleans." She measured 400 tons, and was owned and constructed by Mr. Fulton; she sailed from Pittsburg in December 1812 and arrived at New Orleans about the 24th of the same month. This vessel continued to run between New Orleans and Natchez, the voyages averaging about 17 days, until wrecked near Baton Rouge in 1813 or 1814 by striking a snag on an upward-bound passage."

Another—" the "Comet," built at Pittsburg—a stern wheel steamer of twenty-five tons, with a vibrating cylinder, made a voyage to Louisville in the summer of 1813, descended to New Orleans in the spring of 1814, made two voyages thence to Natchez, and was sold and her engine put up in a cotton gin." CHAPTER VIII.

JOSEPH SOMES. AMONG the great shipping firms of the early and middle parts of the century, we must accord a prominent place to that of Mr. Joseph Somes, as he owned, numerically, a far larger fleet than any of his contemporaries.

As soon as *Lloyds' Register* was published in its present form (1834), Joseph Somes entered many of his ships in its book, ships of all sizes and—in homely language—of all sorts, from the little " Perseverance," of 423 tons, built in Quebec in 1801 and employed whaling in the Southern Seas, to the stately "Earl of Balcarras," of 1,488 tons, a magnificent teak-built Indiaman, formerly running in the service of the Honourable Company.

He traded almost everywhere, to the East and West Indies, to the Brazils, New South Wales, Malta, Lisbon, the Mauritius, &c, &c, and many of his ships were taken up by the Government as transports, freight and store ships, and also as convict I ships.

The convict ships of the early and middle parts of the century, were not usually of the class of vessel which caters in modern times for Government requirements. They were hired usually at a low rate, so low that the better ships were practically debarred from the contracts, and the regulations concerning the surveys were not only lax but easily evaded. So notorious had the evils of the system become, that a special Parliamentary Commission was demanded to enquire into them, with a view to lessen the awful mortality prevailing, and to mitigate in some degree the horrors of the passage. As a consequence of the attention of the Government having, early in the century, been drawn to the transportation service, certain reforms had already been introduced, one of the principal being the employment of naval surgeons in the ships. However, here I have not the space to digress on the subject of convict ships beyond their bearing on the ships and firms of which I am treating.

An excellent illustration was presented to us, not long since, when an old convict ship, built in the last century, was exhibited with all her gruesome apparel, in some of the principal English ports. Possibly some of my readers may have seen her, and though the visit could hardly be regarded as pleasurable, it doubtless had the effect of bringing forcibly to one's mind, the revolting harshness to which those unfortunate creatures were subjected, during their passage out to Australia and subsequent incarceration there.

This, however, was no imputation on the shipowner, his province merely was to supply a ship of sorts—what particular sort depended upon the terms of the charter and his conscience. Among the convict ships, of course, were many staunch and stout, those of Joseph Somes being usually above the average, tendering for this particular class of work.

As some sample rates paid to him for this service may be of interest, I append some:—

In 1840. Tons. Per ton

As the century advanced, so did his fleet improve, and many new vessels, built to his order, were added to the list. Before we go on to his later ships, I will mention a few of the better known of his earlier ones, of which many will probably be familiar,— the " Maitland," 648 tons, built in Calcutta in 1810; the " Bengal Merchant," 503 tons, built in Calcutta in 1812; the " Fairlie," another ex-East Indiaman, built also in Calcutta the same year; the "Moira," 650 tons, built, 1813; the "Lord Lyndoch," also a Calcutta built ship (built, 1815); the " Dunvegan Castle," 446 tons, built in Chittagong in 1819; the " MountStuart Elphinstone," 611 tons, built in Bombay, 1826. I have picked out these few, from many, as being among the best known. Many had previously been running in the service of the H. E. I. C. Besides several of the above-mentioned ships, was the wellknown "Earl of Balcarras," and many will remember her in the middle of the century, sailing for Joseph Somes. She was built in Bombay in 1811; reference has been made to this famous old ship in a previous chapter. Also the "Thomas Coutts," 1,334 tons, built in London, 1817; the "Abercrombie Robinson," 1,425 tons, also built in London; the " George the Fourth," built in London, 1825; the "Java," to which I have devoted a special chapter; the '' Lord Lowther," 1,425 tons, built in London in 1826, &c, &c

Dating from the "forties" were the "Maria Somes," built in Yarmouth, 786 tons, a good sized ship too, as most ships went in 1841; the "Princess Royal," the "Castle Eden," " Sir George Seymour"; and by the "fifties" he had a fleet of fine high-class ships; among the best known being the " Merchantman," built in Sunderland and measuring 1,018 tons; the " Harkaway," 773 tons, built in Dundee in 1852; the "Peeress," about the same size, built in Sunderland in 1859; the "Tyburnia," 1,027 tons, built in Glasgow the same year; the "Europa," a London built ship of 841 tons, also the "Eastern Monarch," one of the finest merchant vessels ever launched, which claims the honour of having been visited by Her Majesty the Queen. She registered 1,844 tons and was built in Dundee in 1856. On her passage home from India with invalid troops in 1859, caught fire and was burnt at Spithead. The most admirable discipline prevailed among the soldiers, who, together with the crew, numbered about 500, and though many of the former were helpless invalids, all were saved but 8.

Dating from the "sixties," by which time nearly all the smaller and inferior vessels had been disposed of, were the "Silver Eagle," 903 tons, built in Troon, 1861; the " Clyde," an iron ship built by Stevens of Glasgow; the "Star of India," a very well-known ship in the Indian trade, 1,045 tons, built in Dundee in 1861; the "Northampton," 1,173 tons, built in Glasgow, 1866; the "Leicester," 1,309 tons, also built in Glasgow the following year; the "Leander," 866 tons, also Glasgow-built in 1867; the "Salisbury," 1,145 tons, built in Troon in 1866; the "Fire Queen," 776 tons, built at the same place in 1864; the "Gainsboro'," an iron ship of 998 tons, built in London in 1866; the "Hereford," built in 1869 at Glasgow, 1,593 ! d " Railto," built in Sunderland the same year. Following the career of this fleet, it is especially noticeable how frequently Government employment was secured.

Eventually the old firm of Joseph Somes was known as the Merchant Shipping Company, and the connection was kept up with some of the wooden ships, reinforced by some fine modern iron ones. Later on, following a consistent policy of keeping the fleet up to date, other modern iron ships were added,—the " Peterboro'," a handsome ship of 1,740 tons, being the best known.

In 1884 one of the old ships had an extraordinary experience in Madeira, and some of us probably have some recollection of it. A full account appeared in the *Times* afterwards, which I take the liberty of quoting.

A correspondent writing to the *Times* from Madeira, under date December 4th, says:—" In 1884, the Pleasure Sailing Yacht Company chartered a ship named the "Tyburnia" for a trip to different parts of the world at the rate of a guinea a head per day. The Yacht on arriving at Madeira a fortnight ago, was anchored near the Loo Battery in the Quarantine Ground, and was ballasted with goods, such as cement, &c, which might yield a profit at the various ports touched at.

"Owing to a misunderstanding with the Portuguese Custom House Authorities, on account of their system of extortion, Captain Kennaley was informed that his ship would be seized and confiscated, whereupon he told them that when the Portuguese officers attempted to board his ship, they would be flung into the sea.

"The Military Governor then gave orders to fire upon the Yacht when she attempted to leave the moorings. Captain Kennaley, who had successfully run the American blockade thirteen times, did not fear the threat and, being assured of the confidence of his passengers, made sail at 8-40 A.m. and, getting her head round the fort, fired two blank charges. As soon as she was under weigh the fort fired at her with ball, carrying away some ropes on the bowsprit. The passengers, both ladies and gentlemen, declined to go below in spite of the continuous firing from the fort, many balls from which dashed the spray over those on board, though no loss of life ensued. The British Ensign was dipped as each shot went singing by, and the Yacht proceeded to Barbadoes."

Truly, an extraordinary experience for the passengers.

This old ship latterly was owned in Australia, and was often to be seen there with many other old liners, discharging lumber from the Sound. About ten years ago, she wended her way to Townsville, Queensland, to take up her last resting place as a hulk for transhipment cargo. When I last saw her there, although her decks had been cruelly maltreated, a large donkey boiler erected between the masts, and her state rooms stripped and converted into storerooms, &c, there were still to be seen around the transoms, &c, indications of departed glory in the remains of the moulding and tattered remnants of the luxurious crimson velvet coverings of the couches.

So much for the "old timer."

There is a well-known tradition concerning the flag flown by these ships, it resembled an Ensign and, so the story goes, was a concession to Mr. Joseph Somes in return for the great services rendered by his firm in time of need.

We will now turn to the eventual fate of some of his best known ships. The "Earl of Balcarras," as detailed in Chapter III, ended her days as a hulk on the west coast of Africa. The fates of the "Abercrombie Robinson," "Thomas Coutts," " Lord Lowther," " George the Fourth," &c, are recorded in the same chapter; and of other early ships, the " Perseverance," mentioned in the early part of this chapter, was broken up about 1841. Space will not permit my detailing many fates, though the loss of the "Lady Nugent" will always be well remembered in connection with the Madras Cyclone of 1854, in which she foundered with four hundred native troops on board. She was built in Bombay in 1813 and measured 535 tons. At the time of her loss she was not the property of Mr. Somes, having been sold to Mr. Haviside.

Let us pass on to the more modern ships. The "Merchantman," built in Sunderland in 1852, was sold in India about 1873 and became a "country ship. " She was always regarded with great interest when she lay at her moorings in Calcutta, and her owner, M. H. Doss, continued her upkeep liberally. She foundered about twenty miles from False Point in 1884. The "Europa," built in 1851, was burnt in 1854. The " Peeress " was sold out about 1879, and having again changed hands, was eventually run into and sunk by H. M. S. "Canada" in 1887. The "Silver Eagle" was eventually sold to Norway and 1 renamed "Aquila." She was built in Troon in 1851. The "Star of India," one of the finest of them all, built in Dundee the same year, was also sold to the Norwegians and eventually, when timber laden, foundered in the North Atlantic, 1893. The " Leicester," built in 1867, was wrecked on the Moluccas in 1877. The " Fire Queen," built in 1864, was wrecked off Madras the following year. The "Salisbury" and "Rialto" were sold to the Germans, and the "Northampton" went in the same direction. Thus closed a famous old line.

CHAPTER IX. THE GENERAL SCREW STEAMSHIP COMPANY. HP HIS was a line, the failure of which has never ceased to puzzle me. They started with most excellent ships, built of iron, at a period of great prosperity—1853, when cargo was plentiful, freights high, and steamships few.

One line ran to India, calling at Cape de Verde, Ascension, the Cape of Good Hope, Mauritius, Point de Galle, Madras, and Calcutta; the same ports homeward with the addition of St. Helena. Another went to Australia, calling at St. Vincent (Cape de Verde) Port Phillip, and Sydney.

In addition to this they had a coasting service from the Cape of Good Hope to Port Natal, and at one time ran a mail from Point de Galle to Mauritius.

Their vessels were built in London, of the highest class, had good power, and, according to the fashion then, were heavily ship-rigged: for, in point of fact, most steamers at that time engaged on distant voyages were but little more than auxiliary, and their steamers were equal in every way to any then afloat.

With this in view, I have often wondered why, when this Company got what we might call the "thin end of the wedge in," they did not succeed in establishing themselves in those trades mentioned.

They did not succeed however, the hand of fate being against them, and first one line was withdrawn, and then another, and the ships scattered; some of them were chartered by the Galway line in the late "fifties, " and in the early "sixties " they were taken over by the East India and London Shipping Company; but such improvements were being made in the marine steam engine, both with regard to lessening the space it occupied in the ship and to reducing the consumption of coal, that their engines had become obsolete, and the end of the "sixties" saw most of them, with their machinery removed, running as sailing ships.

In 1853 they despatched their first ship to the Colonies, arid I append an advertisement of the following year, which gives one some idea of the magnitude of their operations *A dvertise-*

*ment.*

Steam to Australia and India.

"General Screw Steam Shipping Company."

Indian Line.

The Company's line of first-class screw steamers leave Southampton on the 14th and Plymouth on the 15th of every month for Calcutta, with the mails, touching outwards at St. Vincent (Cape de Verde), Ascension, the Cape, Port Louis (Mauritius), Point de Galle, Madras and Calcutta, and at the same ports on the homeward voyage with the addition of St. Helena.

South African Line.

From the Cape to Port Natal every month, in correspondence with the outward and home-. ward bound steamer to India:—

The " Natal," 680 tons; "Cape of Good Hope,". 680 tons; "Sir Robert Peel," 320 tons.

*A advertisement*—Contd.

Australian Line.

Outward to Port Phillip and Sydney direct, touching at St. Vincent only, and homeward by Cape Horn This service, which has been so successfully commenced by the "Harbinger" and "Argo," will in future be maintained by the following first-class iron screw steamships:—

"Harbinger," 1,000 tons. I "Jason," 2,500 tons.

"Croesus," 2,500,, "Golden Fleece, 2,500,, "The Prince," 2,700 tons.

One of these steamers will leave Southampton for Port Phillip and Sydney the first week in every alternate month

Rates of passage money £ 35 to £ 80.

Full particulars may be obtained at the Company's Office;

1, Adelaide Place,

London Bridge.

J. L. O'be1rne, *Secretary.*

They certainly commenced their line to the Antipodes under favourable auspices, for even their little ship " Hellespont" on her way out took 60 passengers and upwards of,£300,000 in specie and jewellery, the fares ranging from 30 to 100 guineas. This ship, by the way, was sold to the Melbourne and Sydney Steam Packet Company for,£20,000.

In July 1854 the General Screw Company accepted the proposal of the Mauritius Government to keep up a monthly communication between Mauritius and opened the line.

About this time an agreement was concluded for the conveyance of mails to Australia once a month, by the establishment of a packet to run once in two months from Southampton to Australia, alternately with the existing line of packets from Singapore, in connection with the Indian service.

But prosperity did not continue; the lines did not pay, and on the outbreak of the Russian War, when the services of every available steamship were then of incalculable value to the British Government, most of their vessels were taken off their lines and chartered to the Government, at profitable rates, to take out troops and stores to the Crimea.

The "Golden Fleece," " Jason," " Indiana," " Propontis," &c, performed good service there; but misfortune seemed persistently to follow the Company's operations.

They incurred immense expense over the burning of the S.S. " Mauritius" while in dock at Southampton and destined for the Crimea. She was most severely damaged.

Again the "Croesus," of 400 H.-P., while in the service of the Government was burnt in the Mediterranean, and the "Prince," of 2,700 tons, the finest steamer of their fleet, was wrecked, November 1854, during a heavy gale in the harbour of Balaclava. The loss of this ship,besides being an almost overwhelming blow to the Company, was a national calamity. She contained (I quote the work of General Sir Ed. Hamley) "everything that was most wanted—warlike stores

Ceylon

The "Propontis of every description, surgical instruments, guernsey frocks, flannel drawers, woollen stockings and socks, boots, shoes, watch-coats,—in short all that the foresight of the Government could devise for the comfort and equipment of the troops. All these treasures went with her to the bottom of the sea."

One hundred and forty-four perished in her, and while the monetary value of her cargo was upward of half a million sterling, the material loss felt by our Army through her wreck can hardly be sufficiently realised.

The earlier ships of the General Screw Steamship Company had been built for the South American trade as their names indicated, but the later names were mainly taken from the mythical voyage of Jason in the "Argo" inquest of the "Golden Fleece." Their eventual fates will, I think, be followed with interest.

The "Argo" was wrecked in 1859 when running in another service.

The "Calcutta," having passed through the hands of the East India and London Shipping Company, was converted into a sailing ship, and re-named the "Darling Downs." She sailed excellently and was a good sea-boat.

To her sailing qualities I can confidently testify, as on a passage home from Sydney, she passed the ship in which I was then sailing, although the latter was well-known both in the Australian and China trades as a smart ship. The "Calcutta," or as we should now call her, the "Darling Downs" was built in 1854, as a steamer of 300 horse-power, under the name of "Portugal."

First as a steamer, later as a sailing ship, she ploughed the waves for 33 years, until she was run *into* and sunk off the Nore by a steamer in 1887, and thus terminated the career of this grand old ship.

The "Golden Fleece," built in 1854, after many (changes of ownership, foundered off the coast of Glamorganshire on a voyage from Cardiff to Alexandria, laden with coal.

The Hydaspes," built in 1852, foundered in the Channel in 1880, after colliding with a sailing ship.

The "Jason," built in 1854, was wrecked in 1863.

The "Lady Jocelyn" (whose original name was "Brazil ") had a successful career, and a less tragic, ending.

She ran for many years, after her machinery had been removed, as passenger ship to New Zealand and was a very popular vessel. She was fitted up a few years ago with refrigerating machinery and is used, I believe, still in connection with the frozen meat import trade in the Docks.

The "Queen of the South," built in 1852, also ran through successive changes of ownership and name. She was launched as the " Milford Haven"—. a steamer of 300 horse-power. She came to her end in 1885, when owned in Liverpool and re-named the, "Malta "; she was wrecked on the coast of Jersey, U.S.A.

The "Mauritius " also underwent many changes of ownership, and in her time flew many house flags. Her name was changed to " Russia," and, like others of the General Screw Steamship Company's fleet, proved an excellent sailing ship. About 1890 she was sold to Norway and so passed out of the register.

The fates of the "Croesus" and "Prince" have already been given, There were also several smaller ships, amongst others the "Cape of Good Hope," which subsequently became the property of the old Calcutta and Burmah Steam Navigation Company, of British India fame, and was eventually sunk in the Hooghly by collision.

To have commanded one of the General Screw Steamship Company's Steamers was, to a certain extent, a Hall Mark, and their Captains' names were soon seen in other employments Among others were Captain Sceales, who afterwards commanded the European and Australasian Royal Mail Steamship "Australasian;" and Captain Douglas, who afterwards became Harbour Master at Melbourne on a salary of,£2,000 and a residence. So ended a most ambitious project and a very fine fleet f CHAPTER X.

DUNCAN DUNBAR.

ACCORDING to the *Gentleman's Magazine,* 1862, old Duncan Dunbar came to England towards the close of the last century, and established before his death, in 1825, a large ship-owning business. Duncan his eldest son, born 1804, was educated at Forres and became a partner in his father's business in 1823; dying suddenly in London, April 6th, 1862, he left property behind him to the extent of a million anda-half sterling.

This colossal fortune was built up mainly in the Australian and Indian trades, and for the latter his ships were exceptionally well adapted, a large proportion of them having been built of teak in India, many in his own yards, for up to the latter end of the "fifties " he enjoyed a considerable reputation in connection with his dockyard business. The enormous amount of cheap-built shipping turned out about that time in North American yards however depreciated his works to a great extent, and the development of steam and of the iron sailing ship soon rendered Indian ship-building no longer profitable. For years were to be seen the ruins of his works and docks in Moulmein, and up to a very recent date the old dock gates were lying there neglected and mouldering away. Early in the century some of his ships had been chartered as transports and some even as convict ships, though it is but justice to the Dunbars to state that their worst ships were not necessarily tendered for that service.

Early in the "forties" they commenced naming their ships after celebrated British battles and probably many, even of his older vessels are within the recollection of some of my readers. The "Bussorah Merchant," built in Calcutta 1818; the "David Malcolm," built in Moulmein 1839; the "Marion," built in Calcutta 1834,—684 tons, which, after a career full of work and usefulness in the Eastern and general trades, was placed in the Atlantic trade and was eventually wrecked off Newfoundland, in 1877. Fortythree years isn't a bad age for a ship to be "punching" across the Atlantic, and speaks well for her teak timbers. The "Cressy," 720 tons, built in Sunderland in 1843, and the " Hyderabad," built in the same year. In 1844 were built the " Poictiers," 756 tons; the "Agincourt," 669 tons, and " Phoebe," 578 tons, all Sunderland built ships. In 1845 the " Trafalgar," 715 tons; "Blenheim," 808'tons, and "Ramilies," 757 tons, all North country built ships, were added, and in 1846 the " Aboukir" of 816 tons. In 1847 the "Camperdown," 993 tons; " Collingwood," 743 tons; both built in Sunderland, and the " Lady MacDonald," of 678 tons, built in Moulmein, were added; and in 1848 the " Minden," 916 tons, and "Waterloo," 898 tons, both Sunderland built ships. In 1849 the "Nile," of 763 tons, was launched at Sunderland.

In the "fifties," the Rodney," 877 tons; "Phoebe Dunbar," 704 tons; "Talavera," 916 tons; "Canterbury," 789 tons; " Pyrenees," 832 tons; "Vimiera," 1,037 5 "Octavia," 1,055 , " Dunbar," 1,167 tons; "Duncan Dunbar," 1,374 tons; " Gertrude," 948 tons; "Lady Ann," 745 tons; "Salamanca," 891 tons; "Sultana, " 775 tons; "Violet," 561 tons, and "La Hogue," 1,331 tons were launched at Sunderland for him, and the "Albuera," 852 tons; "Hougomont," 962 tons; "Cospatrick," 1,119 tons; "Lincelles," 904 tons; " Maida," 519 tons; " Morayshire" and a little vessel, the "Forres" of 293 tons, were all built at Moulmein; the "Ballarat," 713 tons, at Aberdeen; "Northfleet,"951 tons, at Northfleet, and the "Vittoria," 848 tons, and Copenhagen,' 876 tons, were also India-built teak ships, and he also acquired two North American built ships.

During the Crimean War his ships performed yeoman service, conveying troops and stores, and on occasions, the French Mercantile Marine not sufficing for the transport requirements of their own troops, the Government of that country were constrained to charter British vessels for the purpose, and Duncan Dunbar through our own Government, tendered the "Hougomont," already referred to. Although in every way a splendid ship, it was obvious that a name recalling such an association was eminently unsuitable to a vessel about to carry French troops. So, with the consent of Mr. Dunbar, the British Government caused her name to be altered to "Baraguay D'Hilliers" and under that name she conveyed a regiment to the Baltic On the conclusion of the war her original name was restored to her.

On the death of Mr. Duncan Dunbar the ships were sold and, of course, soon dispersed.

The "Albuera," built in 1854, was sold to Mr. Willis of London, and after 21 years' further work in his service, was posted as "missing" on a voyage from London to Tuticorin in 1884.

The " Blenheim " foundered in 1859.

The " Blervie Castle " was lost in the Channel with all hands on a voyage from London to Adelaide in 1857.

The " Ballarat," built in 1852,after several changes of ownership, was sold abroad.

The "Cospatrick," built in 1856, was sold and re-sold, and was eventually burntat sea in 1874 on her passage out to Auckland. The loss of life was awful, no less than 469 perished; the survivors, six in number, were picked up nine days later after enduring the greatest privations.

The "Camperdown," built in 1847, was sold and. re-sold, and at last, when owned by Haley of Sydney C. B., she was run down in the Atlantic in 1883 by theS.S. " Iowa."

The " Dunbar," one of the finest of them all, was built by Laing of Sunderland in 1854; she had a between deck height of 7 feet 3 inches, her poop was 82 feet long and her teak masts weighed—the foremast eight tons and the main-mast nine, and she cost upwards of,£30,000.

This ship is best known in connection with her fearful fate, being wrecked off Sydney Heads in 1857, when outward bound from England and her journey's end but a few miles from her. It is supposed that her captain, anxious to get inside as the weather was becoming threatening, decided to attempt to enter the harbour at night,and unfortunately mistaking the "Gap" for the opening between the Heads, drove ashore on an almost sheer wall of cliff and all on board, save one, perished.

An account of the wreck as given by this survivor was printed in the *Nautical Magazine,* December 1857, which I take the liberty of reproducing.

The account given by Johnson, the sole survivor, was as follows:—"She made Botany Bay August 20th and then sail was shortened to close reefed topsails. The mizen top-sail and spanker were taken in. About seven in the evening Sydney Light was seen, the weather being squally with thick rain; the captain and chief officer were both on the poop. It was raining hard and the light was only seen at intervals but distinctly. She stood along the coast until they had fetched the light up into the lee mizen rigging (about 11 p.m.). All hands were then piped up by the boatswain to wear ship. She was however kept away and the foresail reefed, and she ran in on a heavy sea. It was now blowing fresh in squalls with thick rain. The second and third mates, with the two look-out men, were stationed on the forecastle, when the captain sang out—' Do you see anything of the North Head?' the officer replying that he saw nothing of it. Shortly after this the second mate sang out; 'Breakers ahead.' The helm was then put down and the yards braced up sharp— about two minutes after she went broadside on to the rocks."

As soon as the news reached Sydney, many persons proceeded to the wreck, public vehicles were engaged, and hundreds, notwithstanding the state of the weather, proceeded on foot to the scene of the disaster—six miles from Sydney.

An awful spectacle presented itself before their eyes. The waves, agitated with the fury of the storm, threw the mutilated bodies of the dead upon the rocks—now bearing them back into the deep, and now hurling them back again upon the rocks. An active search to rescue and guard whatever might be floated to the shore was commenced, but the violence of the surf prevented their approaching the scene of the wreck. A large quantity of goods, broken and scattered, were cast upon the shore; some were articles of dress. There was also a piece of crochet work with the needle and reel of cotton attached; a number of children's toys; and a small hat with a feather in it, recognised by Johnson as having been worn by a child on board the "Dunbar" in the tropics. There were also found a few fragments of dress with the names of the owners.

The wind was E. by S.

Could any account be sadder? I think not.

The "Duncan Dunbar," built in Sunderland in 1857, was sold, and later on was wrecked on the Las Rocas shoal. She left London on the 28th August 1865 bound for Sydney, calling in at Plymouth, and on the 7th October, struck on this dangerous reef at half past eight in the evening. Every effort was made to get the ship off; cargo was discharged and upper masts cut away, but to no avail. Pumping was continued until all hope of saving the vessel was lost. Captain Swanson was successful in getting all his people, numbering 117, safe on shore. Eventually they were taken off by the Royal Mail Steamer "Oneida. "

The "La Hogue," built in 1855, was acquired by the well-known firm of Devitt & Moore, and was for long, one of the crack Australian liners. Her accommodation was exceptionally good, and her poop, 97 feet long, extended right up to the-main-mast. There was really hardly any upper deck as she had a forecastle deck and a large house to still further contract its limits. She was one of the last merchant sailing ships afloat, I believe, to carry a single topsail yard, and though at the fore and main she had the usual double yards, the single topsail was retained at the mizen. Her arrival in Sydney was the subject of as much public interest as that now caused by the latest crack "P. & O." or "Orient" liner. A few years ago she was taken to Madeira to end her days and is now at Funchal, a mere hulk.

The "Lady MacDonald," built in 1847, was sold with the rest of the fleet, and was eventually wrecked at Port Elizabeth in 1869.

The "Lincelles," after about 20 years further service for Mr. John Allan of London, was sold to Razeto of Genoa about 1883.

The "Maida," built in 1857, was afloat when I kst visited Brisbane, usefully though humbly employed as a coal hulk, and is towed on occasion alongside of steamers.

The fate of the "Marion" I have already given.

The " Minden " was sold with his fleet.

The "Nile," built in 1849, lasted exactly forty years. She eventually foundered in the Gujf of St. Lawrence on a voyage from Quebec to Cardiff in 1889.

The "Northfleet" was rundown when at anchor off Dungeness in 1873. She was. outward bound to Tasmania, and at about-half past (en at night, when the emigrants were all asleep belofy, she was crashed into by a steamer and went down, very shortly. The steamer proceeded on her way, paying no heed whatever to the victims, and it was pot until some time afterwards that suspicion fell upon, a Spanish steamer, the "Murillo," which had arrived at Antwerp with her bows damaged. Upwards of 300 perished.

The " Pyrenees," built in 1851, was lost in 1855.

The "Rodney" was wrecked on Kenn Reef, Queensland Coast in 1858, and as llustrating the dangers incurred by sailing ships voyaring from Australia to India, through the Torres Straifp route forty years ago, I reproduce the account of the wreck given by the *Nautical Magazine* of that date.— ,i # British ships "Rodney," "Sea Park" and "Northumbrian" left Melbourne together, May 22nd, for Torres Straits and India. On the 6th we were joined by the Dutch barque "Olivier van Noord" to keep company with us through this dangerous passage. All four ships hoisted their longitudes at noon of that day which corresponded to a mile. The course to be steered was then agreed to by all. When I went to bed at 10 o'clock, the "Rodney" was the headmost ship, the "Northumbrian " a little on her starboard quarter, "Sea Park" right astern, and the Dutchman Astern of us. All went on as usual until 4-30 a. m. When I was awoke by the ship being brought to the wind. I jumped on deck immediately and saw what I supposed was the "Rodney " firing blue lights and rockets as fast as she could. We all felt certain that something must be the matter, but could see no danger. The Dutchman passed under our stern as we rounded to, continuing the same course. After looking most anxiously to leeward for some minutes with opera glasses, I saw a faint line of broken watfcr not a mile off on our lee beam. Not knowing which way the reef might run, the ship's head was then kept to the south and west until the day broke when the wind freshened very considerably. We then discovered two vessels on the reef, the Dutchman on her beam ends, with her decks to the sea, which was making a clean breach over her; her position was indeed an awful one; the other, about a quarter of a mile to the eastward of the Dutchman, proved to be the "Rodney" which was comparatively in an upright position; but the rollers which were increasing every moment and broke upon her weather beam, sending the sea high over her lower yards, lifting her for the time and causing her to lurch over to seaward, showed every instant to be precious as there was no knowing how long she might hold together."

The crews were taken off and housed eventually, the "Rodney's" in the "Sea Park " and the Dutchman's in the " Northumbrian."

The " Sultana," built in 1854, ld d resold over and over again, and was at last posted as " missing " on a voyage from Havre to St. Thomas' in 1882.

The "Talavera,"-built in 1850, was wrecked in 1855

The " Trafalgar," built in 1845, on a voyage from Havana in 1860, sprung a leak in the Atlantic and on examination it was found that the destructive worm Teredo Navalis had completely honeycombed her bottom. In spite of all efforts the leak gained on them. In their extremity, fortunately two ships hove in sight and took off the crew numbering 26. She foundered a few minutes after they had been taken off.

The "Waterloo," built in 1848, fetched 4,555 at her sale in 1862. She was eventually sold to a native, Hajee N. Mohammed of Bombay.

The " Vimiera," built in 1851, was sold and re-sold, eventually (1887) passing into the hands of the Norwegians.

And thus, ship by ship, they played their final part.

## CHAPTER XI.

## THE EUROPEAN AND AUSTRALIAN ROYAL MAIL COMPANY.

AFEW years ago, by an odd coincidence, there were lying in the Victoria Docks, London, two old vessels, sold and resold over and over again. One was the Telegraph steamer "Calabria," the other the sailing ship "Oneida." But few people reflect that these two vessels, then lying so close together, once formed part of a line, which in 1857 took over the Australian branch of the P. and O. Company's traffic

Several companies had essayed the Australian steam trade. The ill-starred Australian Royal Mail Company; the General Screw Company; the Australian Auxiliary Steam Clipper Company had all been launched upon the market with the best possible expectations, but after a short struggle, had severally come to grief, the P. and O. alone surviving.

But the circumstances of the Crimean War requiring the services of nearly all the available P. and O. steamers, the conveyance of the mails reverted once more to sailing ships. The uncertainty, however, attending the passages of even the swiftest of the clippers, decided the Governments of the various Australian Colonies to take steps to establish another system of steam communication between England and Australia. Melbourne, before her final measures were taken, having been no less than 108 days without advices from England.

In 1856 the Home Government, at the request of the Colonies—as soon as its attention was free from the distracting influences of the Crimean War—advertised for tenders for the Australian mail service.

The P. and O. Company tendered, their offer being to carry the mails—a monthly service—for an annual subvention of,£14.0,000.

But a new company forming for the purpose, tendered the same service for,£185,000 and, owing probably to the feeling engendered in the Colonies, due to the P. and O. Company having temporarily withdrawn their steamers from the trade, the contract was given to the new company.

It is but justice to the former company to mention that the steamers, thus withdrawn, were of the utmost value to the Government at that time, as they were employed transporting troops, &c, to the war.

In fact, the supply of steamers was so inadequate, that many sailing ships were chartered in addition, both for the conveyance of stores and troops.

The new company commenced business at once; two large iron steamers were acquired, the "European" and "Columbian" of about 2,400 tons and 400 H.-P., built on the Clyde in 1855, both steamers of high class and good speed.

The contract was, as above stated, for,£185,000 from Suez to Australia - *via* Aden and Point de Galle, a large sum and one which in modern days would have guaranteed an efficient service. The route, though offering great interest to the traveller, was in many respects an inconvenient one. After proceeding from London to Alexandria, one disembarked and journeyed across Egypt to Suez *via* Cairo. These stages were performed, partly by boat, for the old canals were utilised, and the River Nile also as far as it served, and partly by coach, horses or donkeys, the baggage, which necessarily was much, limited,, being borne across the desert on the back of camels or dromedaries.

There were rest houses at intervals along the route and hotels at Cairo, but though much could be done to alleviate, nothing could remove, the discomforts of the journey, and its frequent changes of conveyance.

Moreover one's heavy baggage had to go by freight ship, which added to the expense, and had, of course, to be despatched considerably in advance.

In 1858 the railway from Alexandria through Cairo to Suez was opened, and not only shortened, but materially added to the comfort of the journey, saving the above mentioned continued change of conveyance. How few passengers, going through the Suez Canal in our stately liners, reflect on the ordeal of the overland route of 40 years ago.

The " Oneida" of 2,300 tons and 440 H;-P., built by Scott of Greenock, was next purchased and placed upon the line and then followed the "Australasian" and "Tasmanian,"—steamers built expressly for them.

The "Australasian" was built by J. and G. Thomson ship-rigged, had two funnels and was altogether a very imposing looking vessel; on her trial trip she realised 14 knots,, so great things were expected of her as she went out, commanded by Captain.Sceales, late of the " Golden Fleece " of the old General Screw Line, to take up her station between Suez and Australia.

The results from this Company did not, however, fulfil expectations. In spite of the heavy subsidy, the first year's working was unfortunate.

Enormous sums had been spent on their plant in the outports; even the ships did not run with the regularity demanded of them. In June 1858 we read they incurred a penalty for delay in bringing home the heavy portion of the Australian mails. Their capital was soon spent, and then they fell heavily into debt. The shareholders were in despair, and efforts were made to come to an arrangement with the Royal Mail Steam Packet Company for the better working of the service in future. The West India Mail Company's people came to their assistance, but nothing could save the doomed company. They struggled manfully, but eventually liquidated the same year (1858.)

Although the majority of the shareholders were business-men, the Directors do not appear to have possessed the requisite experience in the management of steam ships. Be that as it may, the losses on this venture were ruinous.

One cannot help thinking, that, considering the passenger traffic then prevailing to the Colonies, the few saloon passengers and the enormous expense of sending goods overland across the desert, that smaller and less expensive vessels might have sufficed.

The Peninsular and Oriental Company's directorate, who knew well the requirements of the service, had previously been carrying it on, and successfully too, with considerably smaller vessels.

To return, however, the mortgages were heavy and the sacrifices, consequent on the disposal of the steamers and plant, were enormous.

It had been a bold undertaking and we cannot but admire the enterprise of the promoters. After liquidating, the assets being soon valued and realised, the steamers were quickly scattered.

The "Australasian " was taken over by theCunard people, and ran for some years in the Atlantic trade under the name of "Calabria"; she was eventually converted into a Telegraph steamer.

The "Tasmanian " was taken over by the West India Royal Mail Company, and was a successful and favourite ship for long after, being eventually wrecked at Porto Rico in 1878.

The "Oneida," a bought-in ship, was previously owned by the Canada Ocean Steam Navigation Company, and after the failure of the European and Australian S. N. Company, she ran in the service of the West India Royal Mail.

When they had done with her she was re-sold, and in 1875 converted into a sailing ship. In 1894, however, the Sailing-ship Oneida Company voluntarily woundup, and she was again sold, to become a refrigerating hulk on the South American coast. She must have been a good ship, for even at that age, nearly forty years, she is said to have fetched,£3,250.

The " Columbian" was acquired by the P. and O. Company. She was built in 1855 by Simons of Glasgow. The P. and O. Company sold her to Hadji Cassim of Bombay, who put her in the country trade,, and she was broken up but a few years back. She enjoyed the reputation for many years of being the oldest steamer in the Indian trade.

THE BLACK BALL LINE. OF all the interesting phases of shipping, the era of the clippers appeals to me the most strongly.

The early China and American clippers

have already been dealt with in Chapter XV; but as a regular line to Australia, the famous Black BaU Line stood pre-eminent in the "fifties "and "sixties" for fast clippers and " record " passages.

The names of some of their vessels are still byewords among the shipping world and will, I trust, remain so for many years to come; such names as the "Marco Polo," "James Baines," "Champion of the Seas," "Donald Mackay," "Whirlwind," "Fiery Star" and others equally famous.

The discovery in 1851 of gold in Australia, gave an enormous incentive to prospective settlers; the reports of the gold finds, in most cases greatly magnified, appealed to the venturesome as nothing else could have done.

Australia and its gold fields were pictured as an El Dorado, and people from all parts of the world flocked to the Colonies as fast as the ships could carry them.

"Canvastown" is probably yet in the memory of many of the old "Colonials"; the people arriving in such shoals, and the adventurers on landing immediately making a bee line for the diggings, encampments rapidly became townships.

To my mind there is something not only romantic, but pathetic in these beautiful clippers arriving crowded with hopeful emigrants for the golden land, and this feeling will, I think, be shared by every one who has been engaged in carrying out emigrants to Australia.

At this time it was no uncommon thing for the whole of a ship's crew, on arrival in Melbourne, to desert and make their way to the gold fields, in fact it was almost physically impossible to restrain them, for so keen indeed was the feeling, that leaving often their entire kit behind them, they would escape ashore from the ships on planks or in tubs and have even been known to swim ashore during the night, although the harbour, then as now, swarmed with sharks.

Not only sailors, but mates and even captains often left their ships, which thus frequently lay for weeks wholly denuded of their crews. Then it was when a vessel was loaded and about to proceed to sea that the "fancy" prices came to be paid to sailors for the run home. *£10* and *£1$* a month were often scoffed at, and cases are known when as much as *£go* and.£100 have been paid to each able seaman shipped for the run home.

Those were the halcyon days for poor Jack, though it was doubtless as quickly spent as ever in the "saloons "of Ratcliff Highway and the neighbourhood.

But to return to the Black Ball Line. In 1854 Messrs. Baines secured also another very important contract, that for the conveyance of the entire emigration from England to Tasmania or Van Dieman's Land, as it was then termed, and accordingly arrangements were made for the despatch of a ship every month to Hobart direct.

In May 1855, a contract was entered into for the conveyance of the whole of the Australian mails twice every month, sailing from Liverpool. A reference to the chapter on the European and Australian Royal Mail Company gives the reader a fair idea of the circumstances under which the mail service reverted to sailing ships.

Between 1854 and 1856, many ships were chartered to go out to the Crimea with troops and stores, and at this time other trades were so depleted of large ships, that the following notice was posted up in the Underwriter's room at Liverpool, November 12th, 1855:— "The Government emigration to Australia will, it is feared, have to be given up from Liverpool from shipowners not tendering their vessels for the service."

Many traditions are still current of the old "Black Bailers" and are, and will be, passed on from one generation to another; of the ships driving along in squally weather, the skippers "hanging on" to the last moment; the watch ready for a call, standing grouped together under the lee of the house on deck, and speculating which sail or spar would "go" first; of standing by the halliards throughout the whole watch; of the captain's padlocking the maintack, which in most merchant sailing vessels is of chain, a mute defiance which was well understood. But their captains were well selected, and among the best seamen of their day; having due regard to the safety of the ship and passengers, their business was to "make a passage," they did so and with such success that the Black Ball clippers have become proverbial.

Homeward these ships brought the successful digger and the successful storekeeper, more of the latter however than of the former; for usually it was not the digger who made the money, rather it was the individual who purveyed to him, who supplied him with his provisions, his "bacca," his mining implements and his liquor, and also those enterprising persons who provided him with the means of transport across the country to and from the gold-fields.

In addition to this, as previously stated, the Black Ball ships frequently carried the mails, and a great quantity of gold.

Among the most famous were four ships built by Donald Mackay of East Boston: the "Champion of the Seas," "Lightning," "James Baines" and "Donald Mackay." The "Lightning" came over in March 1854 little over 13 days and the " James Baines " in September of the same year in 12 days 17 hours. This vessel measured 2,275 tons, and was in every way a magnificent ship. In May 1855 she arrived in the Mersey from Australia, having made the voyage out and home in 5 months 10 days. She carried what is never seen nowadays, a moonsail—a small sail set above the skysail; was very heavily sparred, and was 243 feet long by 44 feet beam. At the time of the Mutiny she was taken up by Government with many other crack ships to go out with troops, and was then commanded by Captain MacDonald. Her Majesty the Queen honoured this ship with a visit on the occasion of her departure in 1857.

The following year, most regretably, this fine ship was burnt in Huskisson Dock, Liverpool, on her return from Calcutta. Her fame had been so bruited throughout the land, that her loss was regarded, and with reason, as a national disaster. At the time of her loss, ship and cargo were valued at,£170,000.

The "Champion of the Seas," another equally well known ship, was taken up to convey troops to India about the same time as the " James Baines."

She also was a big ship for those days, being 1,947 tons. After a successful career under the Black Ball flag she was sold, and passing through many vicissitudes, eventually foundered in the North Atlantic, guano laden, in 1870, when owned by Mr. A. Cassels.

Another was the celebrated "Marco Polo," built in St. John's in 1851, she was a three-decked ship. of 1,512 tons, and though but what is known as a six-years ship, was very strongly built. How her massive beams and knees would have dismayed the present day stevedore. In 1853 she made the passage, Liverpool to Melbourne, in 76 days. She took out besides a valuable cargo, 648 passengers and,£90,000 in specie; she beat the steamship "Antelope" this year to Melbourne. Voyage after voyage this ship made between the mother country and the Colonies. In 1861, owned by Messrs. Bell and Lawes, she made the passage, Liverpool to Melbourne, in 61 days. Captain Labbet of Brisbane once told me that in January 1867 he took passage home in the steamship " Great Britain." The " Marco Polo " left at the same time and was soon lost sight of. A week later, the look-out man of the " Great Britain" reported a sail right ahead, and shortly afterwards expressed his belief that it was the " Marco Polo," in which ship he had previously sailed; his opinion was, however, scoffed at. On being neared, he proved to have been right.

She was again distanced and the "Great Britain" made what was esteemed a good passage. On taking the pilot off Cork, the first question asked was: "Have you seen the " Marco Polo?" The reply came, "Yes, she passed up 8 days ago." She had made the passage in 76 days. She was 188 ft. long by 40 ft. beam.

What paying cargoes they bore too; on one occasion the " Montmorency" arrived, her passenger accommodation full up and her holds also, besides,£100,000 in specie, and a little later the " Red Jacket" arrived at Liverpool with 126 passengers, nearly 100,000 ounces of gold and a full cargo. On a former occasion the Black Ball clipper "Lightning " had arrived from Melbourne with;£ 560,000 on freight, succeeded the following day by the "James Baines" with no less than,£700,000.

The majority of the vessels of this firm were, however, soft-wood ships, and did not endure as the British oak-built ships did. Many of them had previously been American clippers running between New York and San Francisco during the great California gold rush, and their reputations were made before the English acquired them. Others were built in the United States and St. Johns, &c, especially for this line.

But the deadly blow launched at the carrying trade of the Northern States by the depredations of the "Alabama," "Florida" and other commerce destroyers produced a panic there, so much so, that ships were transferred wholesale to British registration, and in most cases their names were changed.

The " Tornado," of 1,721 tons; the "Golden Age," the "Neptune's Car," the "Royal Dane," late "Sierra Nevada"; the " Light Brigade," late " Ocean Telegraph"; the "Rockhampton," late "Morning Star"; the "Fiery Star," late "Comet" and many others were transferred to our Mercantile Marine, and when we remember that the " Alabama " alone destroyed nearly sixty fine vessels, the claims on which we had to pay upwards of fifteen million dollars, we can well appreciate Brother Jonathan's haste.

Some of the old advertisements well indicate the class of vessel which appealed to the travelling public *A dvertisement.*

The Celebrated A1. yacht-built clipper "Young Australia," Commanded by G. Phillips, Esqt Came Out in 84 days, to sail positively on the 15th November. Full or not full.

Wool 1. per. lb. in full.

Another advertisement of their large auxiliary steamer the "Great Victoria" is interesting. I culled it from the *Moreton Bay Courier* (now the *Brisbane Courier)* of that date.

*Advertisement.* 1866.

Steam from Sydney to London.

To families and passengers for England. The magnificent Black Ball auxiliary screw steamship "Great Victoria," 4,000 tons burden, R. Richards, Esq., Commander, will sail positively 10th April from Sydney to London.

The superb deck saloons are for elegance, comfort and general arrangements, unequalled by any other ship in the Australian trade, and superior accommodation in the second saloon, intermediate and steerage. An experienced surgeon accompanies the vessel.

*Rate of passage money from Sydney—*

Saloon £ 60 and £ 65.

Beds, bedding, linen and every requisite, except wines and spirits, supplied for £ 5 extra.

Second cabin £ 35. Steerage £ 18.

Third,, 25..

Apply to Br1ght Bros. & Co. or to

Mr. James Baines, the best known partner of the firm of Baines, Grieve, Mackay and Taylor, died, I am told, comparatively poor, but the recollection of his name is still green in Liverpool and several of his commanders are yet alive. Let me express a hope that some of the old gentlemen will come across this book. Some years ago I shewed my note books to Captain Sargeant (of Messrs. Potts, Paul and Sargeant of Sydney and elsewhere.) In his younger days he had been chief mate of the Black Ball clipper "Fiery Star." This ship left Moreton Bay homeward bound, April 1st, 1865, and the *Nautical Magazine* in the September number of that year gives the following graphic narrative:—

"The "Fiery Star," Black Ball Line of packet ships, Captain Yule, left Moreton Bay for London, April 1 st. The fire was discovered on the 19th when one of the crew, named Adams, came aft and reported a strong smell of smoke in the forecastle. The Captain and Chief Officer (Mr. Sargeant) went forward and found the smoke coming up in clouds from the lower hold. Every hatchway in the ship was immediately battened down and the ventilation stopped as far as possible. They were at this time running free, and were about 400 miles from Chatham Island. On the next day a steam pump was set to work on the hatchway and several sails were cut down from aloft to secure the hatches. At 6 p.m. the fire broke out through the port bow and through the waterways on deck. The boats were immediately got out and the captain, officers and passengers (with one exception) and most of the crew got into the four boats. We should here mention that two of the boats belonging to the ship had been destroyed a few days previously by a heavy sea which had struck them. Those in the boats took chronometer, sextants, charts and compasses with them. The chief officer, Mr. Sargeant, seeing that the boats could not possibly hold all on board, gallantly volunteered to stand by the ship and four A.B.'sand thirteen boys followed his noble example."

Seventy-eight men left in the boats and Mr. Sargeant endeavoured by all means in his power to subdue the fire, and succeeded—in spite of the noxious gases—in getting up a chart and compass from the cabin. He set a course to get into the track of ships and encountered much bad weather. On the nth of May having been on the fire twenty-one days, they spoke the " Dauntless," which ship took them all off. When they left, the foremast was almost burnt through.

The merchants of Auckland subscribed £ 160 as a testimonial and presented,£80 to Mr. Sargeant and *£9,o* to the crew.

The fate of the old "Black Bailers " when other firms held the reins of the trade will, I am sure, be followed with interest. The "Duke of Newcastle," 992 tons, built at Quebec in 1862, was sold and was eventually wrecked at Valencia in 1876. The " Southern Empire," late the " Jacob A. Westervelt," 1,418 tons, one of the old three-decked clipper packets, built in New York in 1849, after being sold, foundered in the North Atlantic, 1874, when guano laden. The "Young Australia," 1,020 tons, built at Portsmouth, U.S., in 1853, was wrecked on Moreton Island in 1872, wool laden. The "Conway," 1,195 tons, built in St. John's in 1851, was sold and at last foundered in the North Atlantic in 1875 when owned in Bristol.

The celebrated clipper "Royal Dane," 1,615 tons late the American ship "Sierra Nevada," a three-decked ship, built at Portsmouth, U. S., in 1854, was sold. She was eventually wrecked while on a voyage, Huanillos to Falmouth, guano laden, on the Coast of Chili, 1877.

The "Wansfell," 777 tons, built in St. John's in 1853, was wrecked about 1869. The "Utopia," 948 tons,-built in New Brunswick the same year, was sold in 1866 and abandoned at sea the following year. The renowned clipper "Donald Mackay," 2,150 tons, built by Donald Mackay of East Boston, was one of the famous "quartette. " She was 257 ft. long by 46 ft. beam, and 29 ft. 5 inches depth, her poop was 112 ft. long. She was sold to Mr. Barlling of Bremerhaven eventually.

The "Light Brigade," late "Ocean Telegraph," 1,495 tons, was built at Medford, U. S., in 1854. After being sold and re-sold, she eventually was converted into a coal hulk in Gibraltar where she now lies. I saw her and went on board not long since, about the latter end of 1896. The " Fiery Star" we have already alluded to. The " Everton " ended her days in the South Pacific. The "Landesboro," 1,006 tons, built in Medford, U. S., in 1852, was sold. Her name, when under American ownership, had been the "Morning Star." She eventually foundered on a voyage from Samarang to Falmouth in 1879.

The " David Mclver," 862 tons, a New Brunswick built ship, being sold, was eventually posted as "missing " on a voyage, Quebec to Greenock in 1872. The "Morning Light," a huge clipper of 2,377 tons, built in New Brunswick in 1855, after a succession of ownerships, passed into the hands of the Germans who re-named her "J.M. Wendt"and so into oblivion. The " Shalimar " was disposed of to a Swiss firm. The "Schomberg," a magnificent ship of 2,400 tons, built in Aberdeen in 1855, wrecked on Cape Otway. Her passengers, numbering 430, were all saved. Many yarns are even now current of her commander, Forbes, and his daring efforts to make a passage. He was tried for the loss of his ship and acquitted.

The "Blue Jacket" was eventually burnt. The "Ocean Chief" was abandoned at sea in 1868. The "Queen of the Colonies," 1,346 tons, built in Boston in 1853, was one of the fastest ships of a fast fleet. On two consecutive voyages she made the passage out to Brisbane in 76 days. After being sold, she was eventually wrecked on a voyage from Java to Falmouth, on the dangerous rocks of Ushant in 1874. The "Bayswater," another of the old American three-decked clipper packets, built in New York in 1847, after being sold, eventually foundered in the North Atlantic about 1876 when guano laden. Space does not permit of my detailing all their fates. Most of them, after the Black Ball line gave up, wandered into the guano or coal trades; open fields for open vessels. The "Legion of Honour " was wrecked on the Tripoli Coast in 1876 under other owners, while the famous " Marco Polo," 1,512 tons, built in St. John's in 1851, was afterwards sold to the Norwegians. Frapped in with chains, this once celebrated ship struggled to and fro across the Atlantic, until in an evil hour she was wrecked on the bleak shores of Cape Cavendish, Prince Edward's Island.

Her end is a fitting finale, I think, to this chapter.

## CHAPTER XIII.

## "A FORGOTTEN COMPANY," THE QUEENSLAND STEAM NAVIGATION COMPANY OF 1861.

A NOTHER Company, which had a hard struggle against fate, and to which keen rivalry and reduced freights caused it finally to succumb, was the Queensland Steam Navigation Company.

The Australian Steam Navigation Company of Sydney had the inter-colonial trade, especially that between the Colonies of New South Wales and Queensland, to a great extent in their own hands, and consequently, both fares and freights kept high. As they had worked up the trade themselves, they not unnaturally, looked upon any projected opposition as a positive intrusion upon their privileges, and one may remark *en passant* they charged accordingly.

In 1860 much dissatisfaction was openly expressed at the state of the Australian Steam Navigation Company's Maritime arrangements, although the fares between Brisbane and Sydney had been somewhat reduced, the return fare at this time between those two ports was twelve guineas.

The outcome of it was that a Committee was formed by a few enterprising gentlemen for the purpose of forming a Company to run from Brisbane to the Northern Ports and *vice versa.*

The prospectus appeared in the issue of the *Moreton Bay Courier,* September 22nd, 1860.

*Prospectus.* QUEENSLAND STEAM NAVIGATION
COMPANY.

Capital......,£25,000 in 2,500 Shares of *£o* each.

The promoters of the Company have entered into arrangements with the Government dependent on the formation of a Company for the conveyance of the Mails for a period of 3 years from April 1st, 1862.

It is proposed to order in the first instance, one paddle wheel steamer, to be built expressly for the trade and having all the latest improvements. As it is anticipated that the working expenses, including fuel, will be little in excess of the mail subsidy and that the goods and passenger traffic will be considerable, there can be no doubt of the immediate success of the undertaking viewed as a profitable investment, *etc.*

The first Committee of the Queensland Steam Navigation Company will be—

Gibbon. Raff. Taylor. Coxen.

Munce. Fleming. McDougal. Warry,

Bentley. Burts. Harris.

McAlister. Kent. Raff.

Thorn. FitzSimmons. Stephens. 1 W

A very plausible prospectus.

The almost immediate result was a substantial reduction in the rates of freight and passage by the Australian Steam Navigation Company's Steamship "Clarence " going North.

The shares were well taken up, and then came an interval during which the Queensland Company placed the order for their steamer with Messrs. Barclay, Curie and Company, of Glasgow, and in 1862 she came out. She was a paddle wheel steamer measuring 309 tons and 120 H.-P., and was placed on the berth for the Northern ports with much enthusiasm.

The Australian Steam Navigation Company, determined apparently to brook no opposition, lowered their fares and freights to about half of those which obtained before the New Company's steamer "-Queens, land " had taken up her station

In August of that year (,1362) the rates stood as, follows —

On August 20th a spirited letter was published by Mr. Warry in support of the Queensland Company, deploring the strenuous rivalry of the Australian Steam Navigation Company, and urging the people of Queensland to support their own line.

The half-yearly account was audited, September 27th, and we note a few extracts.

The total cost of the " Queensland " was.£18,930 *14s. nd.* including all expenses up to the time of her being placed on the line.

Her gross earnings for 6 trips from 10th June to:— *£ s. d.*

August 30th 3,168 6 o

Expenses...... 2,107 9

Leaving a surplus of 1,061 5 3

"The Directors have reduced the fares and freights to what they consider an equitable rate, and consider the time has now arrived when it is advisable to increase the capital of the Company to such an extent, as will enable them to place two new steamers on the line between Brisbane and Sydney, a step which they consider will prove a remunerative investment for capital and highly advantageous to the Colony."

"It was deemed desirable to extend the operations of the Company by procuring additional steamers, and in order to carry out this object, the capital of the Company should be increased to. £60,090 in 6,000 shares of *£10"*

On the 30th September thus, shortly after the audit of the accounts, a letter was published in the *Moreton jjay Courier* "lamenting the unworthy rivalry of the Australian Steam Navigation Company" and stating that although the Queensland Company had been in existence since March 1861, their steamer had only been running for three months. The wool freights per bale from Rockhampton to Brisbane by the Queensland Steam Navigation Company was now 7/6 and by the Australian Steam Navigation Company 5/-.

In March 1863 a steamer, the "Star of Australia," of 120 tons and 45 H.-P. , belonging to Mr. Byrnes of Sydney, was chartered to run with cargo only; and now the Australian Steam Navigation Company advertise their rates to be % of the original fares and freights.

On the arrival of the " Lady Bowen " it was decided to place her on the Northern line, *viz.,* Brisbane, Maryboro', Gladstone and Rockhampton and to despatch the " Queensland " on the Southern trips.

The war of rates was carried down on the Sydney Line where the same fierce rivalry obtained; the fares between Brisbane and Sydney stood now as follows:—

Next year the Company was reinforced by the arrival of the "Platypus." She, however, made a long passage-out of 204 days.

She left the "Clyde" rigged as a 3-masted schooner, but sailed so indifferently that the Captain put into Pernambuco and had her rigged as a barque.

The 8th half-yearly accounts of this Company, which were issued in May 1865, are very interesting as shewing the small excess of earnings over disbursements.

*Earnings of the Queensland. £ s. d.*

Lady Bowen and Lady Young. 18,381 1 4

Disbursements... 17,711 15 8 £ 669 5 8

So the struggle went on.

By January 1867 the affairs of the Queensland Company were so critical that a Special General Meeting of the. proprietors was convened for the purpose of deciding whether affairs of the Company be wound up or continued, and it was proposed that a call should be made upon the shareholders sufficient to pay all the liabilities of the Company, *etc.*

Many sanguine shareholders, however, held out against the motion to wind up, and shortly after a shareholder urged an energetic canvas for the increase of the capital, the proposal being for an increase of,£50,000 by means of an issue of 10,000 shares (preferential) at *£5* each which would entitle the holders of such shares to a dividend of 10 /,, and a bonus of £ 30 a share from the profits of the Company before the original shareholders are entitled to any dividend or participation in the profits.

At the end of March this year, the half-yearly accounts shewed a profit over and above all expenses of *£670 gs. yd.,* but Mr. Russel stated that he had obtained the opinion of Mr. Martin, Attorney-General of New South Wales, and the opinion was adverse to the scheme of raising money by means of preference shares unless it was carried unanimously by the whole of the shareholders. Notice was then given of a meeting to consider the propriety of winding up the affairs of the Company as speedily as was consistent with the interests of the shareholders.

Still the war of rates went on, both Companies offering in July a rebate of 10 /,, on rates and an additional allowance of 5 / for prompt cash payments.

At the 13th half-yearly report a move was put forward with a view of re-constructing the Company, and it was notified shortly after that the title of the re-constructed Company would be the "Sydney and Queensland Steam Navigation Company." By October 19th, *% rds* of the shares had been applied for.

It was evident, however, to every practical mind that this suicidal policy of rate-cutting could have but one termination and that,—the collapse of the weaker company. Accordingly we are not surprised to learn that many shareholders were in favour of taking advantage of one of the several offers that had been tendered for the purchase of the steamers and eventually, January 1868, the whole of the Company's property was disposed of to their rivals—the Australian Steam Navigation Company—for the sum of,£42,000.

THE CHINA CLIPPERS. SUCH a halo of romance has been spread over the clipper ships of the "fifties " and " sixties" and their famous passages, that few of us can hear even the word "clipper" without a feeling of interest.

The building of fast ships was, of course, a gradual evolution, and it was not until the early "forties" that ships were constructed with the primary object of speed in view.

The China trade"was the first to supply the impetus; the Americans, with their usual acumen, having awakened to the fact that shippers would come to give the preference to those ships which might ordinarily be depended upon to make the better passages home, commenced the building of ships with fine forms and having great sail area.

Our ships, even the best of them at that time, were but a very slight improvement on the old "Tea-waggons," and when the Baltimore clippers arrived on the scene and established a reputation, which they soon succeeded in doing, shippers would scarcely look at us. These ships had a long, yet somewhat low bow, known as the Baltimore bow, which was long perpetuated in the earlier Aberdeen clippers and were very heavily sparred.

Before our ship-owners realised the position, we were actually being ousted from the tea-trade, and it was not until several experimental ships had been built, that we evolved a vessel able to compete with them.

The discovery of gold in California in 1848 gave an enormous stimulus to the building of swift clippers to run between New York and 'Frisco with emigrants, prospectors, adventurers, what you will.

New York, Boston, Portsmouth and Philadelphia vied with each other in the production of most beautiful ships, their size increased, while at the same time their lines were made finer and the freights between New York and San Francisco being up to *£7* and *£8* a ton at that time, and foreigners being absolutely debarred from sharing in the trade, there was every possible inducement for smart passages, and they made them too.

All the way from New York, through the Tropics toCape Horn, a steady beat around, and then all the way up to 'Frisco.

The "Comet," built by W. H. Webb, made this round trip, New York to 'Frisco and back in 7 months and 9 days. She was 1,209 tons was afterwards known as the "Fiery Star" of the Black Ball Line, to which reference will be made later on.

The "Flying Cloud," built by Donald Mackay in East Boston in 1851 of 1,642 tons, is said to have made 433J statute miles in one day—noon to noon—or nearly 377 knots. It is claimed that Lieutenant Maury supported the assertion. Personally, as the Scotch say, "I hae doots." Moreover Maury, whose works I have searched carefully for allusions to this, merely passes on the tale as "'twas told to him." She was a marvellously fast ship and made the passage, New York to 'Frisco, in 84 days.

The "Sovereign of the Seas," built in 1851 by Donald Mackay, received as freight, New York to 'Frisco on her first voyage, $ 84,000. She was a notable clipper too; for next year she made 6,245 miles in 22 days; in 1853 on a voyage from Honolulu to New York (82 days) she ran 3,144 miles in 10 days. She was 2,421 tons, 258 feet long by 44 feet beam.

Her foremast was 89 feet

,, mainmast,, 93,,

mizenmast,,82,,

Her main yard was 90 feet long, and she spread 12,000 yards of canvas.

From San Francisco these ships sometimes returned to New York in ballast, but usually went on to China to the great detriment of our own traders. These celebrated ships actually commanded there a higher freight than their British contemporaries.

I have an account of the Yankee clipper " Surprise" which, having discharged her outward cargo at 'Frisco, made her way to China and loaded tea at Canton for London.

Her receipts for the round voyage, New York to San Francisco, thence to China and thence to London, had entirely paid the cost of the ship and all running expenses, besides leaving a clear profit of $ 50,000. Her freight home from Canton was *£6 a.* ton.

The "Architect," one of the Baltimore clippers, to which reference has been made, on the strength of her reputation, secured in 1854, 1 *Jc&* a ton freight from Canton to London. By this time, however, the British shipowners had braced their energies to meet this powerful competition and launched several clippers. Jardine Matheson had put the "Stornaway" in the trade, followed by the "Cairngorm," built by Hall of Aberdeen. Richard Green had built his "Challenger,"—so the story goes—in a spirit of emulation, highly creditable to himself and most encouraging to his brother shipowners. She was pitted against the American clipper "Challenge" from Anjer home; continuing the story, ship was staked against ship. Be this as it may, Green's clipper beat the American by 2 days, making the passage in 62 days.

The firm of Shepherd & Lidgett had a number of vessels in the China trade, mostly fast vessels, some being built by White of Cowes, the "Heroes of Alma," "Solent," "Chanticleer," &c Temperleys had the " Cissy," "John Temperley," " Epsom " and others.

But pre-eminently may be mentioned the iron clipper "Lord of the Isles," built 1853 by Scott of Greenock, which came to a tragic end, being burnt a few years after;-the "Kate Carnie" of 599 tons, built in Greenock in 1855; the "Ellen Rodgers" of 585 tons, built 1858 at Greenock; the "Falcon," of 937 tons, built 1859 by Steele of Greenock; and the "Spray of the Ocean," built 1854 by Pile of Sunderland. This ship afterwards ran for the Black Ball Line and the "Crest of the Wave," same builders, which won the celebrated race with the Yankee clipper "Sea Serpent."

The great point in favour of the British clippers was, that from the first they were well-built ships and delivered their cargoes, even after a hard run home, in good order, while the American ships were built mainly of soft wood, which though conducing to a light hull, could not for long stand the immense racking strains put upon them when driven in a strong breeze under a heavy press of sail.

The consequence was that the claims on some of the Americans for damaged cargo were both numerous and heavy, and the ships, by virtue of their slighter construction, would not last as long.

The British builders early recognised the value of iron in the construction of their ships, some of those I have mentioned were built entirely of it, while others known as composite vessels had wooden planking over an iron frame, and of these were some of the most successful of the later clippers.

A large crew was carried in these ships, for all sorts of "fancy " sails were set in light winds "bonnets, ring-tails, watersails, &c,"and sail being carried up to the last minute, it was generally handed in a hurry.

The China tea trade was, no doubt, a very lucrative one, not only for the owners of the successful ships, as much as l a ton in addition to the freight being given at one time, as a bonus to the first arrival, but also to the commanders, many of whom afterwards owned ships in the same trade. All through the "fifties" and "sixties" and up to about 1872, the tea races continued. The new "Lord of the Isles," built in 1864; the "Titania," built by Steele of Greenock in 1866; the "Ariel," which ran in the great race in 1866 against the "Fiery Cross;" "Serica," "Taeping" and "Taitsing." Among owners must be mentioned Findlay & Co., Shaw & Co., Rodger & Co., Campbell, Macunn & Co., and others, owners of almost equally crack ships. An account of the great race of 1866 appears later on, there was, however, discussion as to whether the award should not be divided.

The " Serica " also, and the "Spindrift," the latter built in 1867, 899 tons, came to an untimely end two years later. The "Jerusalem" of Aberdeen, built there by Hood in 1867. Messrs. Walter Hood & Co. built some of the most famous of the Aberdeen clippers, including the "Thermopylae" The "Cutty Sark" of London, the "Fiery Cross" (No. 2) built 1860, 888 tons, which up to a year or two ago was still afloat and owned in Norway; reference will be made to her later on. The "Thermopylae " built in Aberdeen in 1869, 946 tons; the "Taitsing " built in Glasgow; the Forward Ho," the " Undine," the celebrated "Sir Launeelot," built in Greenock in 1865, 886 tons, still afloat and running between Bombay and Mauritius, owned by natives; the " Leander," built in Glasgow in 1867; the "Windhover," built by Connell of Glasgow in 1868, 847 tons; the "Ada," the "Chinaman," the "Flying Spur," the " Lahlop," &c

A most entertaining account of the race in 1866 appeared in the *Nautical Magazine* in the number following their arrival. It is so vividly written that we can almost see the ships ourselves tearing up the Channel near the termination of the race.

The ships that started for the race were the

Ships. Tons. Built in Owners.

Ada 686 Aberdeen Messrs. Wade & Co.

Ariel 858 Greenock Shaw & Lowther.

Black Prince. 750 Aberdeen Findlay & Co.

Chinaman... 688 Greenock Park Bros.

Fiery Cross.. 689 Liverpool... T. Campbell.

Flying Spur. 731 Aberdeen Robertson & Co.

Serica 708 Greenock Findlay & Co.

Taeping 737 Greenock Roger & Co.

Taitsing... 815 Glasgow...... Findlay & Co.

The hardest run was between the "Fiery Cross," "Ariel," "Taeping " and "Serica." The "Serica," "Ariel " and "Taeping" crossed the Foo-chow-foo bar together, May 30th. The "Taitsing " starting on the following day.

The "Ada" left Foo-chow-foo on the

6th June; the "Black Prince" on the 3rd June; "Chinaman" on the 5th June; the "Flying Spur " on the 8th June, and the "Fiery Cross " on the 31st May. The latter passed the Light House at Anjer Point on Lately lost, the 18thJune at noon; the "Ariel " on the morning of the 20th; the "Taeping" on the afternoon of the same day; the " Serica" at 6 p.m. on the 26th, and the " Taitsing " four hours later.

At this time the "Ariel " had evidently got the lead, while the "Taitsing," which left Foo-chow-foo two days after the others, had overtaken the "Serica," the "Fiery Cross" heading both by two days. From Anjer they carried good trades to the Meridian of Madagascar. The " Fiery Cross" passed Mauritius on the 30th June, the " Ariel " on the 2nd July.

# # #

On the 9th August, Lat. 12 20'N., the "Fiery Cross" signalled the "Taeping" and continued in company till the 17th with wind variable and light. In Lat. 2752'N., Long. 36 54'W., afresh breeze sprang up which took the "Taeping" out of sight of the "Fiery Cross" in four or five hours. The "Fiery Cross was becalmed and not making one knot per hour for 24 hours. This circumstance is alleged to have lost her the race. On the 29th she reached Lat.415'N., Long. 35 51' W. and at 10 a.m. on the 6th September, she sighted the Isle of Wight bearing N.N.-W. with a wind W. S.-W. blowing hard.

The "Ariel " and "Taeping " which had lost sight of each other for 70 days, on the morning of the 5th instant, at 8 o'clock, recognised each other off the Lizard running neck and neck up the Channel with every stitch of canvas that could be set, with a strong westerly wind.

During the whole day the two ships kept their position, dashing up the Channel, side by side, in splendid style, sometimes almost on their beam ends every sea sweeping their decks. On approaching the pilot station off Dungeness, they each fired blue lights to signalise their position.

At daybreak the pilots boarded them at the same moment, and the race was continued in the same manner until they arrived in the Downs, where they both took steam tug to tow them to the River. The ships had to shorten sail to enable the tugs to come up and pick up the hawsers to take them in tow. This was about 8 o'clock a.m. and the tugs starting almost simultaneously and both ships neck and neck. The "Taeping," however, was fortunate enough to have a superiority in the power of her tug and reached some time before the "Ariel. " The " Serica" followed closely upon them. She passed Deal at noon and got into the River in the same tide which carried the "Taeping " and "Ariel " up the river to the Docks, when the result of this extraordinary race was declared to be as follows:—

Taeping docked in London Docks. 9-45 p.m. Sept. 6th 1. Ariel,,,, East India 10-15 p.m.,, 2.

Serica,, West India,, 11-30 p.m.,, 3.

The " Taeping" was, therefore, the winner of the premium, about £ 500, the bills of lading of each ship setting forth that 10/-per ton extra would be paid to the first sailing vessel in Dock with new teas from Foo-chow-foo. The " Fiery Cross" arrived in the Downs on the 7th, and was compelled to bring up to an anchor on account of a heavy gale blowing when she remained some time. She, however, managed to get into London Dock by 8 o'clock on Saturday morning the 8th, some 28 hours after the "Taeping. " The " Taitsing " arrived in the river on Tuesday forenoon.

But the opening of the Suez Canal, though prophecied by many to be doomed to failure, offered such facilities for steam shipping to the East, that the clippers were gradually relegated to the carrying of inferior teas and finally ousted altogether.

Some of the owners accepting the inevitable went in for steam, and thus in a year or two, the whole trade was revolutionised.

The clippers sought other employments, most were entered for the Australian trade, where their rapid passages upheld their reputation and guaranteed them a homeward wool freight.

The dimensions, and also some of the eventual fates of these clippers, may prove interesting to my readers.

The first " Lord of the Isles" was burnt in the China Seas in 1862; the second one, built in 1864 by Steele of Greenock, was eventually sold to the French and re-named " Paul Albert"

The second " Fiery Cross" was built in Liverpool in 1860; she was 185 feet long by 31 feet 7 inches beam by 19 feet 2 inches, and was eventually sold to the Norwegians.

The "Spindrift," owned by the firm of Findlay & Co. of Glasgow, was wrecked in 1869.

The "Jerusalem " of Aberdeen 901 tons, has also passed from us. *Apropos* of the latter vessel, I remember a most exciting race with the large American ship "Iroquois." We were homeward bound from the Colonies flying light and very crank, a not uncommon condition with a wool cargo.

The "Yank" was first sighted on our quarter, the wind being quarterly, blowing moderately though squally at times.

While the wind remained so, the "Iroquois" had no chance, but when it freshened, the "Jerusalem" heeled over to such an extent, that necessitated sail being taken in. Soon the American was ploughing along to leeward carrying her three top-gallantsails and whole mainsail and going as steadily as a die, while the "Jerusalem " was flying along with fore and main lower top-gallantsails and reefed mainsail, but heeling over to such a degree that one could barely stand upright, the water roaring up through the lee scuppers and during the squalls, lipping in over the rail.

In a short time the top-gallantsails and mainsail were handed, and preparations made to reef the foretopsail. By this time, however, the " Iroquois " had just passed the beam, when, apparently, her skipper satisfied to have passed us, "snugged" his ship down to three reefed top sails, and we shortly after lost sight of her in a blinding squall.

To see this ship, when moderately light, was a great pleasure, her lines were the perfection of symmetry. In one day, I remember, 324 miles being got out of this ship; she was one of the first to carry double top-gallant yards. Her owners, the Aberdeen Clipper Line (Messrs. George Thompson & Co.) afterwards sold her to the Norwegians, and she eventually foundered in the North Atlantic laden with pitch, pine, rosin, &c, on a voyage from New Brunswick to Fleetwood.

The "John Berham," the old rival of Green's "Challenger," also came to her end in the turbulent Atlantic

There was the "Cutty Sark," one of the most exquisite models ever built, she also was for long after employed in the Australian trade. Built in Dumbarton in 1869, she was 212 feet long by 36 feet beam by 21 feet, and measured 921 tons. Her owners, Messrs. Willis, sold her to the Portuguese quite recently (1895). The "Forward Ho" was wrecked in 1881. The famous "Thermopylae," built by Hood of Aberdeen in 1868 for the Aberdeen Clipper Line, usually known in the Australian Colonies as the "Aberdeen White Star Line." This ship, on her first voyage out to Melbourne, went out in 60 days, pilot to pilot, thence she went to Newcastle N.S.-W. to -load coals for Shanghai; from Newcastle to Shanghai she went in 28 days; from Foo-chow-foo to London she made the passage in 91 days, the voyage occupied but 6 months and 3 days. She was a composite ship of 946 tons, was 210 feet long by 36 feet beam by 21 feet and was eventually sold to foreigners, and is, I believe, still afloat.

The "Taeping" was lost in 1873. The "Min," built in 1861 by Steele of Greenock, was sold to Hawaii and re-named the '' W. B. Godfrey." She was wrecked a few years ago on the Australian coast.

The "Sir Launcelot," built in 1865, was 197 feet 6 inches long, by 33 feet 7 inches beam; she is now owned by natives and registered in Bombay, in which port I saw her, looking very smart, a year or two ago. Her best day's work was 354 miles.

The " Black Prince " was lost among the Java Islands, though long after her sale. The "Chinaman" met her fate in the Flowery Land. She was run into by a steamer and sunk in the Yangtse River in 1880. The "Windhover" was wrecked on the Australian coast in 1884, while another well-known clipper, the "Isles of the South," built in 1859 by Laing of Sunderland, 821 tons, was sold to foreigners and re-named "Loining." The "Yangtse " and the "Taitsing" were both lost in 1872,1 believe. The "Falcon" built in 1859, was sold about 1870 to the Austrians and re-named "Sophia Braili." The "Ellen Rodgers" was lost about 1866. She was wrecked in the Java Seas about 1872. The "Guine *Vide* footnote at page xoi.

vere" (No. 1), built in Greenock in 1862 for Messrs. Macunn & Co., who owned some of the best of the clippers, measured 647 tons, and was stranded in 1866, while " Guinevere " (No. 2), built by Randolph Elder & Co. in 1868, was 857 tons register, 197 feet long by 34 feet beam and was eventually sold to foreigners. The celebrated '' Taitsing " was wrecked on the Zanzibar coast about 1883.

Thus ended the days of the clippers, and though but little trace is left of the ships and the sentiment excited at the time—fast dying out, yet as long as our national shipping exists, the romance of the ships and their marvellous passages will never be forgotten.

CHAPTER XV. THE AUXILIARY STEAMERS. IT is difficult now, looking back at the steamers of the "thirties," "forties" and "fifties," to differentiate between the so-called full-powered and the auxiliary vessels; indeed, well into the "sixties," steamers employed on distant voyages, such as to the Australian Colonies, New Zealand, India, &c, were so heavily ship-or barque-rigged as to be, in a great measure, independent of their engines. Coal was procurable at but few places abroad, and owing to the high freights generally prevailing—very costly; there was not, also, the confidence in the engines we see now; and he who suggested that any steamer of such date should depart on an ocean voyage without spare sails, spare topmast or even spare topsail yard, would have been indeed deemed a rash man; thus these two cogent reasons, the expense of coal and the lack of confidence in the engines then felt, doubtless accounted for the long retention of the lofty masts and heavy spars carried even on the more fully powered steamers.

The earliest Atlantic steamers were auxiliary vessels, that is to say, sailing vessels which utilised their steam power merely as an auxiliary to their sails, in calms and light winds, coasting, going in and out of port, &c, and many of the voyages described in the chapters devoted to the pioneer steam lines were performed in this way.

The idea sounds plausible enough even now; a vessel which can perform her voyages almost as economically as a sailing ship and at the same time is raised from the helplessness of the latter, in calms, by being able then to utilise her steam power, surely should make her passages in infinitely less time than a sailing vessel, and at the same time command a readier cargo and enhanced freight on account of the regularity of her arrivals. But in practice it has not been found so; the screw for example, when sailing, even when allowed to revolve, was a certain "drag" on the vessel and when hoisted up, took up much room and the great aperture thus left in the run of the ship seriously interfered with her manoeuvring powers under sail.

Again, the engines, boilers and coal bunkers occupied much space which could otherwise have been profitably filled with cargo, or utilised as passengers' cabins, and the engine room staff—though employed but seldom—still had to be paid and housed and fed.

One of the earliest and most interesting experiments—an auxiliary as distinguished from a fullpowered steamer—was that of the " Maria," a barque of 460 tons, owned by Messrs. Urquhart and Gardner. She was fitted with two engines of ten horsepower each, and in a calm could make three miles an hour on an hourly consumption of two hundredweight of coal. A great advantage, however, consisted in her being able to raise steam in less than an hour. Under the command of Captain Black, she left for Bombay in 1839.

The results, however, were not startling, the wooden sailing ship then was approaching its zenith, and without some very practical result it was not easy to induce the public mind to follow any problematic advantage.

Another effort in this direction was the "Massachusets," an American packet ship of 750 tons, built in 1845. Her engines of 170 horse-power drove her in calms 9 miles an hour on a daily consumption of 9 tons of coal. Her propeller was so fitted as to be capable of being lifted out of water when not required for steaming. She was the first ship, I believe, fitted with double topsails, and was reputed a good sailer. During part of her eventful career she was in the service of the United States Government, and there proved of great utility.

The early "fifties" saw a great development in the auxiliary steamer, and many companies were exploited about that time,—the General Screw SteamShip Company; the Australian Auxiliary Screw Clipper Company; Lindsay's Auxiliary vessels; the Australian Royal Mail Company, &c, &c

So much was this type of vessel in evidence in the "fifties" and "sixties," that special tracks for the various seasons were plotted out for them, nearly approaching to those followed by sailing ships. The old P. and O. route from Bombay to Aden in the South-West Monsoon is still to be found in many sailing directories; while on the other side of India the brig-rigged steamers of the British India Company, when bound from Burmah to the Coromandel and Madras Ports, would "keep away" until everything drew, then lay, full and by, for the Coromandel side. Fetching up usually between Gopaulpore and Bimlipatam, they would then steam down the coast under the shelter of the weather shore.

But as time rolled on and the consumption of coal proportionate to power exerted and distance traversed, lessened, so the earning capabilities of full-powered steamers increased, and the auxiliary vessel gradually fell back into the rank of the sailing ship. So one by one their machinery was removed, and they became sailers pure and simple.

Besides the ships and firms already mentioned,. between the " fifties" and the " seventies, " auxiliary steamers traversed nearly all quarters of the globe, some owned by the "Companies," some by private owners and some by the Commanders; and a very prominent place should be accorded to Mr. W. S. Lindsay, the shipowner, indefatigable in his efforts to design a compromise between a sailing ship and a full-powered steamer.

The latter gentleman having secured the contract for the Calcutta Mail Service after the General Screw Company had abandoned the field, placed seven vessels on the line.

The route as laid down was from Dartmouth to Cape of Good Hope, Mauritius, Point de Galle, Madras and Calcutta; the remuneration,£41,000 yearly. The pioneer steamer on the line was the " England," an iron full-rigged auxiliary clipper of 950 tons and 100 nominal horse-power; she was reputed to have made *g4* knots on a daily consumption of 14 tons of coal and had space for 1,300 tons of cargo, 180 tons of coal, and 50 first cabin passengers. Her first voyage was a successful one. She took out, we are told, 500 troops for the Cape of Good Hope, a field battery, £ 50,000 in specie, and a full cargo of merchandise. Notwithstanding the favourable auspices under which the adventure was commenced, they were not successful, and after twelve months were withdrawn from the service.

The " England " was afterwards in the China and Japan trades, and was sold to the Japanese Government in 1861. Sometime after she and her sisters, the "Scotland " and "Ireland " of about the same size, and the "Tynemouth" and "Robert Lowe" were engaged to carry out a scheme projected to supply steam communication between San Francisco and China. Shortly afterwards the "England" was employed at the siege of Kagosima, where she was sunk in 1863. The " Scotland" was also sold to the Japanese.

The " Tynemouth " was of a larger size, but, smaller horse-power. The most successful of them all, however, was the "Robert Lowe," 1,250 tons, and 80 nominal horse-power. She made some smart passages in her time, on one occasion (1862) going from Cork to Auckland in eighty-two days, and she established for herself a good reputation with the Government as a fast and commodious troop-ship. In the "good days" she, for a vessel of 1,250 tons, netted some princely freights, realising (in 1863) Hankow to London—.£10,315 for freight alone and,£480 for passage-money. In 1870 she first went through the Canal, but she was, by this time, doomed as a steamer, and the redoubtable old vessel was soon afterwards converted into a sailing ship and re-named the "Iron Cross." She was eventually lost—about 1892, I think.

To return to our theme, the Messrs. Wigram were among the last to employ this type of vessel, but the "compounding " of the engine rang the death-knell of the auxiliary steamer as surely as " tripling" has that of the sailing ship.

It is very interesting to get hold of some elderly engineer whose earlier career has been spent in such vessels (alas! there are not many left now), especially if he happens to be in a communicative mood. Not long since I chanced to make the acquaintance of such a man; his sea-service dated back nearly 50 years, and one of the old gentleman's experiences, with his permission, I here relate.

It seems that he was engaged as a Chief Engineer, being a man of considerable experience, in the "Oberon," one of the last of the auxiliaries. She was built for Messrs. Shaw, Maxton and Company's China trade. Captain Maxton, an old and successful China trade commander, (late of the "Falcon") presaging that the Suez Canal would prove a failure, had her built as an auxiliary screw-clipper to go round the Cape; She was heavily rigged and carried three skysail yards. On her first voyage she steamed down to Plymouth and proceeded thence under sail, steaming only when absolutely necessary. At her best she could do but 7 knots an hour on a consumption of 7 tons of coal daily, but could do nothing against a strong head-wind and sea. On this voyage she carried two engineers, and three firemen. On her second voyage she sailed from Plymouth to Port Said in the short space of 18 days, she then steamed through the Canal and through the Red Sea. Towards the Southern end of the Red Sea, however, they experlenced the strong southerly wind and, being absolutely unable to steam against it, the Captain dropped anchor off Mocha in the hope of the wind lessening. After waiting 8 days and the wind being as fierce as ever, they weighed anchor and, under steam and canvas, beat out, tack for tack, through the Large Strait. By this time, however, she was short of coal and had to put into Aden to procure some, and again on the passage to China had to coal at Labuan. This voyage she had three engineers and three firemen. She arrived too early for the tea season, and in the interval traded on the coast.

While going up the Yangtse River to Hankow on one occasion, she could barely stem the tide which was running nearly 7 knots, and with great difficulty arrived off the Orphan Rock. Here the pent-up current was rushing with such force that the " Oberon" could only just hold her own and could proceed no longer. The Chief Engineer assured the Captain that the engines were doing the utmost they were capable of.

The working pressure was thirty pounds, while the boilers had been tested up to sixty and the Chief Engineer, after due deliberation, jammed down the safety valve, which increased the pressure to fortyfive pounds and enabled her to pass in safety. The affair was noted in the Log Book, and on arrival in London, duly reported to the Board of Trade. *On* her first passage to China she occupied 110 days and on the second 134. Her engines were soon removed and she continued her career as a sailing ship. This ship cost upwards of,£35,000 in 1869 but, twenty-five years later, (1894), her value had so depreciated that we are tcJd in *Fair Play,,* she fetched but £, 2,800 on being eventually sold to the Italians.

Yet it is but fair to state that the experiment of the auxiliary steamers was not given up without a struggle, for not more than fifteen or sixteen years have elapsed since auxiliary steamers were running out to. the Colonies, and a few years ago an, enterprising German shipowner built a large sailing vessel with small auxiliary power. Every known improvement was fitted in her, including water ballast tanks, &c, but no practical lesson could be deduced from this modern revival of an old theory as, unfortunately, the vessel was soon lost. Among the many conjectures hazarded as to her fate, the most likely was one which inferred that the probable emptying or partial emptying of one or more water ballast tanks so reduced her stability that she capsized under, possibly, conditions of wind and weather,, which ordinarily would have caused no alarm whatever.

Moralise as we may, the *pros,* and *cons,* of the auxiliary vessels were well considered in their time; that the compromise was not successful was due to no. lack of ingenuity or forethought and their era, extending over thirty years, presents a phase of shipping no less instructive than interesting.

## CHAPTER XVI. EARLY STEAM TO AUSTRALIA.

T N Chapter 7, especially towards the latter end of it, we touched on the Atlantic companies, and detailed several of those which now have ceased to exist. In this chapter I propose to deal with some of the earlier steam companies to Australia.

The P. and O. were early in the field but, for a considerable period, did not secure a continuous mail contract. As the pioneer steam line to Australia, however, I should certainly name the Australian Royal Mail Company, and I reproduce their prospectus.

AUSTRALIAN ROYAL MAIL STEAM NAVIGATION COMPANY. *Prospectus).*

Capital,£500,000 in 50,000 shares of *j£* 10 each, to be increased as required.

*Dlrectors.*

Wtn. Hawes, Esq., *Chairman.*

Chas. Geo. Barnett, Esq.

Phillip William Flower, Esq.

John G. Frith, Esq.

Capt. F. B. Hankey, R.N.

R. H. Kennedy, Esq.

Geo. Meek, Esq.

John Richardson, Esq.

Robt. Sheppard, Esq.

Ed. Tostal, Esq.

Chas. Walton, Esq.

*Trustees.*

Henry E. Gurney, Esq., Joseph Hoare, Esq. Benjamin Lancaster, Esq.

*Consulting Engineer.*

Isambard K. Brunei, Esq., F.R.S.

It demonstrates the immense advantage to be derived from a steam communication with Australia, &c, &c, and proposes to provide auxiliary screw vessels of about 1,600 tons and 300 H.-P., so arranged as to carry cabin, intermediate and steerage passengers, and from 800 to 900 tons of cargo.

(1.) To establish a bi-monthly communication with Australia by means of 4 large iron screw steamers, touching at the Cape de Verde Island, Cape of Good Hope, King George's Sound, Adelaide and Port Phillip on the way to and from Sydney. This will at once require an expenditure (2.) To extend this to a monthly communication as soon as possible; for this part of the plan an additional £ 200,000 will be required in the course of the 2nd year. (3.) To supply, as experience proves to be expedient,between Australia, the Indian Archipelago and England, and with a view to accomplish such *Bankers.*

Messrs. Barnet, Hoare & Co.

*General plan of the Company.* important objects, it is proposed to take power to increase the capital of the Company to £ 1,000,000. *Estimate of the receipts and expenditure for the first plan.*

Estlmate Of Voyage. *Dr.*

Insurance, ship-s stores & homeward freight per voyage 1,635

Wages, Officers-and crew 2,500

Victualling passengers and crew, excluding wines and spirits.... i,575

Coals 4,500

Port Charges, commission on freight, engine store and sundry payments during voyage...... 2,5

Depreciation and wear and tear, including ship-s stores, &c,... 2,600

Administration, office expenses...... 1,250

Balance Profit 6,618 *Cr.*

By Passengers, 120 out and 120 home—all classes

Freight and tonnage,
700 tons out and 700
tons home

Gold specie and parcels,
out and home

Short freight, pass., &c.
to C. Verde Id. and
Cape of Good Hope,
out and home

Profit on wine, spirits,
&c

Her Majesty-s Mails... 4,233

By profit per voyage,£6,618, or for 6 voyages *£39,*708. Proposed capital. £200,000 for four boats, at 20% = £ 40,000.

Application for shares to be made to Messrs. Sheppard & Sons, 28, ThreadneedleSt., the brokers of the Company, &c, &c, &c

They secured a contract for a two-monthly mail service to Australia and employed five iron steamers:—

The " Adelaide," 1,124 tons and 45 H.-P., built in London 1852; The " Australia," 735 tons and 300 H.-P., built in Dumbarton 1852; The " Melbourne," 817 tons and 260 H. P.," built in Greenock 1849; The "Sydney," 735 tons and 300 H.-P., built in Dumbarton 1852; The " Victoria," 1,120 tons and 450 H.-P., built in London 1852.

In the alternate months the arrangement was to forward the letters to the Colonies by the Singapore route.

In 1853 the " Melbourne" occupied four months on her passage out to Swan River, which hardly conduced to the reputation the Company was desirous of establishing.

Steam ships, though successfully projected across the Atlantic, had scarcely arrived at the stage when a long sea voyage could be undertaken without frequent stoppages for replenishment of fuel, and the reader who follows the remarks in the Chapter on the "Auxiliaries," will readily perceive why such vessels, unless very ably managed and economically worked and further assisted by a substantial mail subsidy, could not hope to compete with the fast clippers of their date. Space does not admit of a detailed history of this interesting venture. It was an up-hill struggle for a share of the Australian trade with expensively worked steamers, against some of the first clippers of the world. I have before me, as I write, a testimonial, dated December 4th, 1856, to Mr. William Chance, whilom Chief Engineer of the S.S. "Sydney" and the letter accompanying it I reproduce.

To Mr. WILLIAM CHANCE, at Messrs. RICHARDSON & SON,

Shipbuilders,

W. Hartlepool.

Sir,

I have the pleasure, on the other side to hand you certificate and good conduct during your employment in the "Sydney," which I trust may be of use.

Enclosed I also band you your testimonials which were lodged in this office. I shall be glad if you will keep me advised of your address, in case of our being able to employ the vessels again.

I am, Sir,

Yours faithfully, MATTHEW RICHARD SCOTT, *Secretary.*

This letter shews the hopeless state of affairs, for, though the outbreak of the Crimean War found remunerative employment for them, such employment was but transitory, and as opportunity offered the ships were sold, and the Australian Royal Mail Steam Navigation Company ceased to exist.

The fates of the ships were exceptionally interesting, and the history of the first mentioned steamer, the "Adelaide," I take the liberty of transcribing from the *Nautical Magazine* of 1871:—

"This ship was built in Millwall in 1852 & registered in London as the " Adelaide " in December of that year. She was sold to foreigners in 1863 and again registered in London as the "Mersey " on the 30th May. She was again sold to foreigners and registered in London, 28th April 1864, as the " New York," and again sold to foreigners and registered in London, 2nd September 1864 as the " Brazilian." She was transferred to the Merchants' Trading Company of Liverpool and re-registered at that port on the 29th October 1869. Since 1869 she has been trading to India and the Mediterranean and is at present lying in the Birkenhead Float, to have new engines and boilers. She has proved to be a strong ship. Her old engines were "compounded " by Jack of Liverpool, and a new description of boiler fitted to her, from the drawings and under the superintendence of Mr. John Jordan of Liverpool."

The "Brazilian" or " Adelaide" battled with fate for eight and twenty years, being finally wrecked in Liverpool Bay in 1880.

The " Australian " and "Sydney " wandered out to India, and for sometime were in the service of the Government. About 1862, I think, the British India Company bought them, or, rather, I should say the Calcutta and Burmah Steam Navigation Company, as it was then termed. They were re-sold eventually to the Egyptians, and I saw one of them in Port Said about 1888 or 1889.

The "Melbourne" was sold and went out to China. Undergoing various changes of ownership and also of route, for during part of her career she was running between Liverpool and New York, she came into the hands of Mr. Bates of Liverpool and was converted into a sailing vessel about 1867. She left Calcutta for Dundee in 1874, and was never heard of again.

The "Victoria" met with many changes, and her extraordinary story I produce from the *Nautical Magazine* also.

The Bolivian" was built at Millwall 1853 and registered in London as the "Victoria "on the 8th April 1853, ld to foreigners and registered in Liverpool as the "Shannon," 4th June 1863; she was again sold to foreigners and registered in Liverpool as the "London "; she was again sold to foreigners and registered in London as the "Bolivian," on the 9th March 1864, and after registry she was sold to the Merchants' Trading Company of Liverpool and placed in the Indian trade. She was considerably altered in appearance under the direction of Mr. John Jordan; she was cut in dry dock in Liverpool and drawn asunder ninety feet, with the intention of lengthening her, and remained in that state for ten months, when she was again put together without any additional length. Since then she was sold and is at present lying in the roads at Charlton to be broken up. *Naut. Mag.* 1873).

Thus the five steamers of this enterprising venture have been accounted for.

While this prospectus was before the public, another Company was being exploited—the General Screw Steamship Company, but for this, however, a separate chapter is reserved.

Another,—the Australian Pacific Steam Navigation Company—was floated the following year under the presidency of Mr. G. Hilbert, as a limited liability undertaking, and 5 iron steamers were contracted for in January 1853. Well indeed was it constructed on the limited liability arrangement, for in less than eighteen months it wound up and the ships were, I believe, purchased by the Messageries Maritimes Company of France.

Another,—the Australian Direct Steam Navigation Company—was incorporated by a Royal Charter, June 24th, 1853, with a capital of £ 1,000,000, in 40,000 shares of £ 25.

The proposed route, which in a modified form, finds more favour now than it did then, was from:—

Milford Haven to Navy Bay 4.552

Across the Isthmus by rail......... 46

On to Otaheite 4,488

And alternately to Sydney and Melbourne... 3,351

Total Distance... 12,437 Miles

Three years later another interesting prospectus appeared before the public—that of the Australian Auxiliary Steam Clipper Company, Limited.

THE AUSTRALIAN AUXILIARY STEAM CLIPPER COMPANY, LIMITED.

Capital £ 250,000 in 10,000 shares of £ 25.

Deposit £ 5 per share.

*Board of Directors.*

John Gillespie, Esq.... London.

Henry Hoffman,,,... Do.

Robt. Jas. Brown,,,... Sunderland.

T. V. Gooch,,,... London.

Emilus Clayton,,,... Brighton.

Joseph Spence,... London.

This Company is formed for the purpose of establishing direct communication with the Australian Colonies, by means of fast sailing clippers with auxiliary steam power to propel them in light winds and calms.

This combination, as proved by recent experiments, will obviate entirely the well known delay and uncertainty which occurs in the case of the present clipper ships, in consequence of calms on the line and elsewhere, as well as the frequent detentions in the voyages of ordinary steamers by failure of machinery and taking in of fuel; at the same time an immense saving is effected by the room, which would otherwise be occupied by coals and powerful engines being made available for cargo.

THE AUSTRALIAN AUXILIARY STEAM CLIPPER COMPANY, LIMITED—*contd.* - The Directors have already received subscriptions to the amount of,£70,000 or,£80,000, and have purchased three vessels, one of 1,470 tons, and 100 H.-P., one of 1,170 tons and 80 H.-P., and one of 1,400 tons and 60 H.-P.

The Directors propose, in the first place, to run vessels from London to Melbourne, calling at Plymouth for passengers, and feel convinced from experience that the voyage can be performed in about sixty days out, and seventy home. It may be mentioned that the only reasons that the respective owners of the vessels have for transferring their property to the Company, is that vessels of the proposed class can be more advantageously worked in a line, to attain which object, they are desirous of obtaining co-operation and increased capital.

Details as to payments of shares follow.

The subjoined statement contains a comparison between a vessel running on account of one of the large steam companies and one now intended to be employed.

It requires a very casual inspection to arrive at the weak and strong point of the two systems, and proves that the proposed vessels will cost only onehalf of the amount of those lately employed, and consume one-ninth of the quantity of coals, yet they THE AUSTRALIAN AUXILIARY STEAM CLIPPER COMPANY, LIMITED—*concld.* will carry three times the amount of cargo, making the passage in less, or at least the same time. Details of the prospectus follow.

The "Istamboul," 1,470 tons O. M. and 2,200 burden, will sail from London and Plymouth, respectively, on the 10th and 15th of November next.

Applications for shares on the accompanying form can be addressed to the Directors at the offices of the Company, 77 Cornhill, City.

The impracticability of the scheme was soon demonstrated. The "Istamboul" was sold and having her engines removed, was re-named the "Turkish Empire." She was built by Pile of Sunderland in 1856.

The " Indomitable," built in 1855, measured 1,041 tons and was of 80 horse-power. She was also converted into a sailing ship and traded for long in the Eastern seas, being lost, I think, about 1869.

The European and Australian Steam Navigation Company, by reason of the magnitude of its operations, has been accorded a special chapter.

The Liverpool and Australian Steam Navigation Company claims more than a passing notice.

They owned the "Great Britain" of early Atlantic fame. She was built in 1843, at a cost of upwards of £ 120,000, but was a most expensive vessel to maintain. Originally she had five masts, but the sail power thus afforded being deemed insufficient, she was re-rigged as a three-masted ship. Probably few vessels have had such a chequered career; a glance at Chapter Seven shews her early history, when running in a pioneer steam service across the Atlantic From September 1846 to August 1847 remained sunk in Dundrum Bay, but apparently suffered no material harm. The son of an eminent shipbuilder in the North of England told me that his father journeyed over to Dundrum Bay to see her, and to satisfy himself by personal observation as to the relative merits of wood and iron in shipbuilding. He returned very much impressed, and his subsequent operations were, doubtless, much influenced by the result of his observations. Not only were her plates infinitely thicker than those of modern vessels, but were "drilled" for rivets, instead of being "punched," as is now, for economy's sake, usual.

About 1883, after forty years as a steamer, this grand old vessel was converted into a sailing ship and eventually, May 1886, on a voyage from Cardiff to Panama with coals, was condemned as leaky off Cape Horn and is now (1897) hulk at the Falklands. She was far from being an economical ship, her engines, of an antiquated type, consumed from 35 to 50 tons of coal per day—1,200 from Melbourne to the Cape of Good Hope, and thus the space for cargo was much contracted.

The next venture of Messrs. Gibbs, Bright & Co., the representatives of the Liverpool and Australian Steam Navigation Company,was the "Royal Charter,"asteam clipper of 2,720 tons burden and 200 horsepower. She was ship-rigged with double topsails and her propeller was so arranged that it could be lifted out of water in ten minutes. She steamed out of the Mersey, making nine knots an hour, with seventy-five revolutions a minute, and a pressure of thirteen and-ahalf pounds. On her trial trip, she made seventy six revolutions a minute, and her coal consumption was estimated at twenty-two tons in twenty-four hours. As I have said, she carried double topsail yards and was the first English vessel to adopt that system. Her main yard was one hundred and one feet long, her royal yard even being fifty feet. Her 'tween decks, three hundred feet long and eight feet four inches high, was fitted for five hundred and ninety passengers, besides the accommodation afforded to eighty or ninety cabin passengers.

Messrs. Paterson of Bristol built the vessel, while Messrs. Penn and Company of London supplied the engines, which were of the "trunk" pattern. Her armament consisted of four 24-pdrs., four 18-pdrs. and a large swivel gun on the forecastle.

Under the command of Captain Boyce, late of the clipper ship " Eagle," she left Plymouth for Hobson's Bay on February the 17th, 1856, and made the passage in 59 days—the "record " run at that date j her greatest day's work under canvas was 352 miles, and the best under steam 252.

Three years later, when on a homeward passage, under the command of Captain Taylor, carrying about five hundred passengers and crew, a valuable cargo and specie to the amount of four hundred thousand pounds, she was wrecked on the Anglesey coast. Thirteen of her passengers had disembarked at Queenstown and when on her way to Liverpool and nearing that port, she was caught in a terrif1c northerly gale, October the twenty-fifth, 1859, and drove ashore in the night. In spite of every effort of those on shore, no assistance could be rendered, and four hundred and forty-six lives were lost. I must mention that about thirty-five people were saved by the heroism of Joseph Rodgers, a seaman who swam ashore with a line and established a communication, while George Swicar the boatswain, was mainly instrumental in saving nine lives at the risk of his own. The services of these brave men were afterwards publicly recognized in Liverpool. In this disastrous gale, known as the '' Royal Charter" gale, upwards of three hundred and forty-three ships were lost. Subsequent diving operations recovered upwards of £ 320,000.

The Black Ball Line owned auxiliary vessels in addition to their fleet of clippers, the best known being the " Great Victoria." She was originally a French steamer, the "Jacquard," built at Nantes in 1854 and measured 2,278 tons. Her engines of 150 horse-power drove her in fine weather one hundred and eighty miles a day. In 1866 she made the passage—Plymouth to Moreton Bay—with six hundred and fifty passengers on board, in seventy-eight days. I reproduce an advertisement from the *Moreton Bay Courier,* relating to this ship.

STEAM FROM SYDNEY TO LONDON.

To families and Passengers for England.

The magnificent Black Ball auxiliary screw steamship "Great Victoria," 4,000 tons burden, R. Richards, Esq., Commander, will sail positively, tenth of April, Sydney to London.

The superb deck saloons are for elegance, comfort and general arrangements, unequalled by any other ship in the Australian trade, and superior accommodation in the second cabin, intermediate and steerage.

An experienced Surgeon accompanies the vessel.

*Rates-of passage money from Sydney*—Saloon £ 60 and £ 65.

Beds, bedding, linen and every requisite supplied (except wines and spirits) for £ 5 extra

Second cabin... £ 35

Third cabin... £ 25

Steerage... £ 18

Apply to:—Br1ght Bros. & Co., or to J. and G. Harr1s, Brisbane.

She was afterwards sold and converted into a sailing ship.

I have not mentioned the P. & O. in this chapter, for they, while companies have come and companies have gone, seem to remain—and deservedly so—unassailable, and this modest work professedly treats but of companies that " have been."

Messrs. Wigram's auxiliary vessels, a few years back, were among the favourites in the Australian Trade. Unable, however, to compete with the more fully powered steamers in the early "eighties," they were sold and their machinery being removed, they became excellent sailing ships; one of them, the "Somersetshire," built in 1867, I saw in the Hooghly about 1896.

She was then owned by the Norwegians and had been re-named the " Prince Edward." Messrs. Wigram however are still, I believe, steamship owners and therefore their vessels, interesting as they were, hardly come within the sphere of this book.

Another enterprise, which excited great interest at the time, was the establishment of a mail communication between England and the Australian Colonies *via* the Isthmus of Panama.

The route was from England to Colon, thence across the Isthmus to Panama, and thence to Wellington, New Zealarid. The latter passage covered seven thousand miles, which meant then about thirty days continuous steaming without a stoppage. The conditions of the Company's tender were as follows: The service between Panama and Sydney to be carried on at 8 knots for a subsidy of,£90,000 per annum, while they offered to conduct it for 85,000 if a seven years contract was conceded. In addition they demanded,£1 10,000 per annum for a 10-knot service between Panama and Wellington, and not less than 8 knots between Wellington and Sydney, and if extended to seven years, to be reduced to 105,000.

The pioneer vessel was the "Ruahine," a twin screw steamer of 1,501 tons and 400 H.-P., soon followed by the " Kaikoura" of the same size and power; the "Rakaia," 1,456 tons and 350 H.-P., and "Materua," 1,767 tons and 350 H.-P. In addition to these were several steamers of smaller size, employed locally coasting and in inter-colonial service; the "Egmont," "Claud Hamilton," &c I reproduce an early advertisement which may prove interesting. 1866.

STEAM TO ENGLAND *Via* PANAMA.

"Ruahine," 1,503 tons, 350 H.-P.

T. S. Beal, Commander, will leave for Panama *via* Wellington, July 10th. The next steamer will leave on the 1st September and after that on the 1st of each month.

Passengers can proceed from Panama to all parts of America, California, Valparaiso and the West Indies, and *via* France to all parts of the Continent.

John V1ne Hall, *Manager.*

The "Ruahine" ran the longest ocean mail voyage which had ever been made without stopping, and was a good advertisement for the full powered steamer and also for the twin screw principle.

To a great extent the Panama and New Zealand Company conducted their operations under the auspices of the Royal Mail Company, the latter receiving the mails at Colon and conveying them to England.

For the first year everything prospered satisfactorily, but soon difficulties and complications arose, and eventually the Company closed its account.

The ships were sold and wandered into other services, and other trades; the "Kaikoura," "Rakaia" and " Ruahine" being taken over by the Royal Mail Company.

The " Kaikoura" was re-named the "Tiber" and was eventually (1882) wrecked at Haiti.

The "Rakaia" was re-named the "Ebro" and, after a period of service with the West India Company, was resold to the Trans. Company, Barcelona, and re-named "Baldomera Inglesias" and is, I believe, yet afloat.

The " Ruahine" was re-named the "Liffey" and was wrecked on the Uruguay Coast in 1874.

I think now that we have reached the chronological limit of " Early steam to Australia." CHAPTER XVII.

THE FATE OF SOME FAMOUS OLD SHIPS.

A1 7" HAT an inexhaustible subject! there is prac » tically no limit to our researches. We grow older day by day, and are slow to realise that the ships of one's boyhood are among the old timers of to-day, and as such, are regarded by the present generation.

Going back, however, to early History, the fate of even the more notable galleys, biremes and triremes of the ancients would not be read without interest, and, pursuing the subject in chronological succession, the end of the more famous of the Viking's ships, so celebrated in song, the "long shyppes," "cogges" and '' snakes " of the darker centuries, and later even the "carracks " and "galleons" of the middle ages, possess an interest to those connected with the sea.

Occasionally we hear of these old Norse galleys being unearthed, several have been found in our own country; an ancient vessel has even been discovered at Berne in Switzerland; and in the far South have been found remains of Spanish galleons. Not long since, a correspondent from Ireland forwarded an account of the remains of some of the ill-fated Armada, which are yet to be seen at low tide on the coast of Donegal.

The fate of many of the ships which bore such valiant discoverers as Magellan, Davis, Tasman, Dampier, Anson, &c, are not easily traced, owing to the difficulty experienced in some foreign countries in obtaining accurate records. The fates of some, such as Magellan's, we know; of others we shall never know.

Some trace, however, is preserved in Oxford University of the "Golden Hind," the ship in which Sir Francis Drake circumnavigated the globe in 1578-1580, in the shape of a chair made from her timbers.

At Cavite, in Luzon, for ages lay the remains of an old Spanish galleon. The date of her stranding has not been handed down, but there is little doubt that she was one of the "tall shyppes " which annually left Manilla for Acapulco, to return laden with treasure. For centuries these ships had roused English cupidity and many and bloody were the attempts to capture them. Usually they endeavoured to escape, but when pursued and brought to bay, being heavily armed and well manned, often showed a most stubborn resistance, as our freebooters had learned to their cost, but one successful capture generally realised enough to maintain the victors in affluence for the rest of their lives.

On the Great Barrier Reef, extending from New Guinea down nearly the whole of the Queensland coast, have been found the remains of these old galleons. From one of them, a few years ago, several guns were recovered, and in order to arrive at some approximate date, impressions were taken of the casting marks and forwarded to Madrid. With great courtesy the Spanish authorities returned the fullest information in their power. From another a considerable amount of silver was recovered, and I have seen photographs of some of the time-honoured coins. There is but little doubt that these ships had run down to the Southward to avoid capture, and eventually either became hopelessly entangled among those intricate coral reefs and shoals and soon struck, or else ran, likely enough in the dead of night, straight upon them and foundered immediately; for though the existence of Australia must have been known to their commanders, charts were vague and unreliable and possibly they had no information as to that great natural wall, the Barrier Reef.

To me there is something more than touching in these old wrecks, these silent mementoes of the past.

It is said that when Captain Cook entered Provi dential Channel in the "Endeavour " in 17.70, he saw a wreck there, but was unable to approach it on account of the heavy breakers. Somebody had apparently attempted the passage before him. Even to Captain Cook, essentially a prosaic man, this must have presented an eminently pathetic picture, alone among these unknown and untraversed seas, and believing himself the first to enter the Channel, this nameless wreck is sighted, of which the clue neither has been nor ever will be, unravelled.

Some of my readers may have been down that perilous coast which, even now, to modern ships provided with the present beautiful and accurate charts, and piloted through those reefs, most of which are now marked with beacons, by men of consummate skill, presents ever an element of danger. How much should our respect be accorded to those early navigators, with their rude and imperfect instruments and erroneous charts, sailing absolutely vaguely over those trackless seas, and how much sympathy with their fate wrapped in such impenetrable mystery.

Another wreck existed on Long Island, Whitsunday Passage, Queensland coast. It was seen by Captain Flinders about the end of the last century, or earliest years of this, and was computed to be about 170 feet long. She was an oak-built vessel and her bolts are described as being of an enormous thickness. Those engaged in examining her were up to their waists in water, and the sharks collected in such numbers that they had to discontinue their investigations. What she was—where she came from—whither she was bound—we shall never know.

While on this subject we may fittingly allude to the " Endeavour." Of this ship, which should have been preserved as a National Memorial, although we have many records of her construction, purchase and original employment, no material trace now exists.

Another vessel of great historic interest was the "Betsey Cairns" in which William, Prince of Orange, came over to this country in 1688. She was built on the Thames early in the 17th century, though the precise date is not known. As to her original name (although many conjectures are hazarded) and earlier employment, we are equally at a loss, although we know she was purchased especially to convey Prince William and his suitc, as bcing a fast and weath erly ship. Just prior to the embarkation she was re-named the " Princess Mary."

King William III afterwards proved himself not forgetful of her services, and though she was even then an old ship, retained her as a Royal Yacht, in which capacity she was afterwards in the service of Queen Anne. At last, sentiment not being a strong point of the Georges, she fell into disfavour, and was sold and re-named "Betsey Cairns. " She ran for many years in the West India trade, and let us picture to ourselves for a moment this "tubby " little vessel, 83 feet 3 inches long by 23 feet beam, a low bow, high stern surmounted by a poop, the break of which as well as the stern being profusely carved, her three "lanthornes" perched high over her taffrail, "punching " across the Atlantic She was brig-rigged and, after the fashion of those days, carried a lateensail on the " Cross Jack " yard.

Another report ran that she was built in a Royal Dockyard about 1690, and that William of Orange came over in a vessel called the "Brill." Personally I incline to the former account, as, step by step, her career has been pieced together.

At last she was relegated to the coal trade, and for years was a well known ship, between the Tyne and London. In 1827 this redoubtable old ship was wrecked on the " Black Middens," near the mouth of the Tyne, and then, and not till then, did people begin to appreciate her historic value, and great efforts were made to save as much as possible of the old vessel. Many of her timbers were recovered and thousands of souvenirs were made of them, while the knightheads were placed in the Newcastle Trinity House. For longevity there is but little doubt the "Betsey Cairns " holds the record.

The " Royal Escape," in which King Charles the Second made his escape from Brighton in 1651, lasted for many years, and up to the latter end of 1819, was a Government hoy or smack; beyond that I have not been able to trace her.

Another vessel was the " William Fane " which, in 1759, carried General Wolfe over to Quebec She was built originally as abomb-ketch—a vessel designed for a method of warfare—which was deemed at that time very effective and continued for a long time; our mortar frigates in fact were a survival. On being sold out of the service she was employed as a merchant ship, and in 1856 came to Bristol and was put in Messrs. Wilmot's Dry Dock. She was found to be in excellent preservation, and, after but little renewal, was undocked. My father saw her then and describes her as being low forward, the bowsprit consequently having great steeve and having a very high and narrow stern and barque-rigged. This celebrated ship was lost three years later in the Mediterranean, while carrying out a cargo of coals.

The old " Kitty " brig, one of the best known coast. ers, was built in Whitehaven in 1764, and measured 130 tons. She foundered on a voyage from Dieppe to Runcorn in 1884, laden with flint. In the subsequent enquiry it was proved conclusively that she was in a good and seaworthy condition, and was not overladen when she left Dieppe. There was, consequently, no direct evidence as to the cause of her loss.

In striking contrast to the verdict given in the case of this stout old last century brig, was that given in the case of a barque, the enquiry on the loss of which was held very shortly after. She was built 112 years after the "Kitty," and was lost the same year, consequently was but 8 years old at the time of her loss, compared to the 120 years of the "Kitty." She encountered very severe weather after leaving St. Johns, causing her to strain and labour so much, that she became water-logged: " Not prematurely abandoned," was the verdict. Our forefathers knew well to build stout ships.

The " Eliza," built in Jersey in 1772, which came to a tragic end, was employed literally for generations as an Atlantic packet ship. Of deep sea vessels of our own time she was unquestionably the oldest, and I wish it were possible to get hold of some of her old log books. When she was two years old, war broke out with the United States of America; and in 1778 with France; with Spain in 1780, and with Holland also the same year; in fact, war was almost our chronic state at that time. Doubtless, though armed, she would seldom leave during those stirring times without convoy, carrying merchandise out and home at war freights. In her declining days she was employed between South America and Newfoundland, bringing fish down and returning with ballast, and it was while engaged in this unromantic pursuit, that the old ship was wrecked.

A contemporary of hers—a Danish ship, "De Tre Sostern," built in Rudkopingin 1772, is yet afloat. She was seen in the Harbour of Kiel quite lately, staunch and sound, in fact, she still carries grain cargoes.

A very old vessel, until recently in the employment of the Dundee Harbour Board, was the little "Antelope." She was built on the Thames in 1798, it is believed for a yacht, and later on was in the pilot service in Liverpool. Subsequently she became the property of the Dundee Trinity House and was employed in the river for marking sunken wrecks. When this work was undertaken by the Dundee Harbour Board, the little vessel was taken over with the plant. She was next sold to Messrs. Powie Brothers, and is yet afloat.

The "Natalia, " or more correctly speaking, "Nathalie " in which Napoleon escaped from Elba in 1815, then by no means a new ship, eventually stranded off Monterey, on the coast of California, and up to a very recent date her timbers were to be seen at low tide.

What links in history these old vessels supply!

Another old vessel was the brig " Brotherly Love," and I quote from an article which appeared in *Fair Play,* June 27th, 1890, evidently contributed by a gentleman to whom the subject was one of great interest:—" One of the most remarkable of the wooden ships I have known was the "Brotherly Love" of South Shields. This was a collier brig and mention was made of her in the series of articles on "Shanties and Sea Songs" in this journal a year or two ago. The " Brotherly Love" was built in the early part of the last century and was owned by the late Mr. James Young of South Shields, who inherited her from his father, to whom the brig descended, I believe, from his father. The amount of tender care which Mr. Young bestowed on this venerable brig was the talk of the Tyne, and her goings and comings were retailed from hand to hand as items of personal news, in which the whole community was interested. She made her voyages between the Tyne and Thames as faithfully and regularly as any of her younger sisters, and, quaint as was her build, there was a business-like air about her, which shewed that the old builders knew what they were after. Never was private yacht more carefully over-hauled, repaired and painted, than was the "Brotherly Love." Mr. Young made a perfect pet of her and "Old Jimmy," as he was called, must have expended her value over and over again on her upkeep. Still she was the pride of his fleet and the Wonder of the port. Her exact age I never knew, but she must have been about a hundred and fifty when she was run down off the Yorkshire coast in 1878. After all it was not nature which over-mastered her, but man's invention in the shape of a steamer."

A very interesting article!

I find, however, that she was built in Ipswich in 1764, and curiously enough, the Mr. James Young mentioned in the article, also possessed the old "Amphitrite," having purchased her about 1872. A correspondent to *Notes and Queries* describes the sale which, to use his own words "resulted in Mr. Young being the possessor of the two oldest ships in the world." Among the company present was, by a strange coincidence, a Mr. Jas. Walker—a gentleman who had formerly been an apprentice on board the "Betsey Cairns."

I find the "Amphitrite" was built in North Shields about 1776, so at that time they could hardly have been the two oldest ships. The "Amphitrite" measured 303 tons.

As recently as 1875 the " Regent," belonging to His Siamese Majesty, on ascending the Trang river in the Malay Peninsula, found, we are told in the accounts of that expedition, a large ship of European build lying aground a long distance up. It is conjectured that she was one of the old Dutch East Indiamen. Nothing is known of her, or of the fate of the crew; it is another of those unfathomable mysteries.

A few coasters there are still existing which were built in the last century, but nothing about them of interest calls for notice.

In a previous chapter I have alluded to the want of interest we display with regard to old ships; when they fall into the hands of such owners as Mr. Jas. Young who loved his old ships, or Mr. W. J. Smith who owns the "Java," and some few other such owners of old vessels, who take a sentimental interest in them, we may be content. The average man, I fear, cares but little, to him a ship is merely a money-making machine, and the older she gets and consequently the more expensive, as more repairs and renewals are necessitated, the less net profit she returns. Newer vessels, measuring less and carrying more, are competing with him in the same trade, and finally the old vessel falls into disfavour, renewals are postponed, and at last if the enterprising foreigner wont buy her, she is either turned into a hulk or cut down into a haul-about or lighter, and her name and associations are soon forgotten, or else he disposes of her to a shipbreaker under whose remorseless hammer and axe the old ship plays her final part.

CPSIA information can be obtained at www.ICGtesting.com
Printed in the USA
BVOW02s1430250214

345965BV00010B/345/P